The Matter of

THE MISDIRECTING MASTERMIND

The St. Louis $50 Million Diamond Heist and Bridge Hostage Caper

Steve Levi
Master of the Impossible Crime

PUBLICATION CONSULTANTS
WE BELIEVE IN THE POWER OF AUTHORS

PO Box 221974 Anchorage, Alaska 99522-1974
books@publicationconsultants.com—www.publicationconsultants.com

ISBN 978-1-63747-065-7
ebook ISBN 978-1-63747-066-4

Library of Congress Catalog Card Number: 2021951142

Manufactured in the United States of America.

Just because something is obvious
does not make it true.

. . . Detective Heinz Noonan

East St. Louis
Friday, July 2nd
High   89°
Low   68°
Precipitation: 0
Humidity: 64%
Wind: 5 mph

CHAPTER 1

Traffic was slow for Friday, July 2nd in East St. Louis. Then again, there was no reason for anyone to be staying in town for the three-day vacation. There was lots of fishing within a day's drive of the city and St. Louis, the "Big City," was just across the Mississippi River. If you happened to be a baseball fan, it was the weekend for the so-called "Game of Century" with the Cardinals playing the Denver Rockies. Within an hour's drive in any direction were scads of museums, nightclubs, coffeehouses and idyllic retreats – not to mention hundreds of swimming pools, public and private. No, there was no real reason to be in East St. Louis on a hot day like this.

George pulled into the parking lot of the Panhandler Hotel and rolled more than drove toward the empty parking space at the end of the lot. He stopped beside the hotel's dumpster and gently put the rusting mini-bus in reverse. Then he backed into a narrow space behind the massive iron canister next to the concrete wall of the Panhandler. It was a perfect place to hide a vehicle in plain sight, even one as large and plain as the old ten-seater. The trash bin masked the bulk of the vehicle except for a tag of the bumper on the front and the top of the logo on the side of the van. The only section of the logo showing were the tops of the heads of the smiling family of four; mom and dad smiling with a little boy holding a bucket of sand over his head and a little girl tossing a red ball into the air. For all intents and purposes the van was hidden. Hidden in plain sight, but hidden nonetheless.

George adjusted his white gloves and straw hat as he limped across the empty parking lot and then alongside the building in the blast of the afternoon sun. Then he disappeared into the dim coolness of the reception area of the hotel.

The Panhandler was one of the nondescript buildings in downtown East St. Louis which reminded the residents just how far they had come. Originally the cement building had been a warehouse, built as a cement box for the Union Pacific Railroad during the Second World War. The structure had been built to withstand a shelling. Why was a good question. The answer was anything built for the military during the Second World War had to be able to withstand a shelling. War front, home front, waterfront, it had to withstand a barrage of cannon fire. After all, no one knew what would happen if American troops could not stop the German advance in Europe or the Japanese in the South Pacific. We could very well be fighting the Germans here in the streets of East St. Louis. Just in case it happened, we had to build for that contingent.

The cannonade fire-proofing was fine with the cement companies. They made their fortunes by the cubic yard. It was fine with the unions as well. More cement meant more trucks carrying the colloid to the job site and more man-hours on the job. These structures would last a century; 80 years later they were still erect and operational. Just not for the purpose they were originally intended.

The Panhandle Hotel was shaped like an oblong box, its stubby side bordering the cracked WPA sidewalk while its length disappeared into the shrubbery of the adjacent vacant lot. Windows, one per room, had been cut into the cement wall and two emergency exits, one for each floor, had been punched through the back wall. Behind the hotel was a high fence separating the hotel from East St. Louis's storm drain system. Derelicts made their home in the network of tunnels beneath the city streets during the summer. When winter dumped 30 inches of rain in four months, the only people in the tunnels were skin divers looking for the bloated bodies of children stupid enough to believe they could outswim the 20 mile-an-hour current under the city.

The air-conditioned coolness of the interior of the hotel hit George like a cool slap across his face. It was a wet slap and steamed his glasses. He pulled off the spectacles and rubbed them on his shirt sleeve. If the clerk at the counter wondered why anyone would be wearing long sleeves on a day like this, he didn't mention it.

"Edwards. You should have a reservation." George's voice was cool and aged. He sounded as old as he looked. And he looked like every other old person in Illinois during the summer: coiffured white hair, modest tan, healthy stature and an accent to indicate he had grown up somewhere in Missouri.

The kid at the counter was new to George. That was fine with George. The fewer people who saw him more than once was good for business. The kid was young, no more than 17. He had a name tag reading "Johnny" but he was more likely a Pedro or Estaban. George had never seen him before but in this kind of hotel, it wasn't much of a surprise. The Panhandler was not exactly the kind of place with long-term employees.

The boy with the Johnny nametag opened an ancient register and looked down a list of rooms and names. "Yes sir, Mr. Edwards. Paid in advance. Three days. Are your other guests with you?"

"They will be here this evening. You have the other four rooms ready?"

"Yes, sir."

George spotted "Johnny" looking at his white gloves with interest.

"Porphyria," George responded to the gaze by raising his hands. "My skin is very sensitive to sunlight. It gives me a rash. So, I wear this hat." George tapped his hat and then his long sleeves, "and the long sleeves." He smiled. "But don't worry. It's not contagious."

"St. Louis is a tough place to live if you're sensitive to sunlight." Johnny smiled. He didn't sound like a Pedro or Estaban.

"So they say," George picked his key off the counter. "Could you give me a wake-up call at 7:30 in the a.m.?"

"Yes sir, Mr. Edwards. Enjoy your stay here in East St. Louis."

George limped down the long hallway to the very back of the hotel. But he only limped until he was out of sight of the hotel counter. Then he slipped the cane into his right armpit and ascended the rickety staircase to the second floor two steps at a time. His room was the last on the right opposite the laundry facility for the hotel and immediately adjacent to the fire escape.

CHAPTER 2

James Elroy Whittaker, the grandson of the first black engineer on the Union Pacific, was at the helm of the **Bonanza** for its maiden journey. While this trip was hardly dramatic in the sense history was being made, it was significant for Whittaker because it wasn't often a 22-year old earned the right to command a $200 million locomotive. He was only hauling three dome cars but, hey!, it was a big deal. To him! He was in charge. Even more important, he had earned the right to be in charge. After all, how many *summa cum laude* mechanical engineering students anywhere in the United States had a second, specialty major in locomotive engineering? There were, in fact, none. Which was the reason James Elroy Whittaker had no trouble getting the top-of-the-line job running the **Bonanza**, the newest most powerful locomotive on any line between St. Louis and Chicago – maybe even as far west as San Francisco.

There were just a bunch of travel writers on board. Once again, who cared? His career had been off with a fine start. He was 22, had a full-time job while a lot of his fellow graduates were interning or starting at the bottom of the bowels in some cookiecutter engineering firms whose names were just letters followed by an Inc.

Then, so to speak, his maiden voyage went off the rails.

CHAPTER 3

For Illinois State Trooper Rachel Rabinowitz, it was just another day of tedious patrol along Interstate 64, all 40.6 miles of it, when the call came in. *Here we go again*, she said to herself – out loud because she was alone in the squad car. *Another dumb job.* She felt like Dirty Harry without any of the glamour. Whenever there was a bottom-of-the-barrel job, she was the one who had to bend over the staves and wallow in the dregs. Welcome to the Illinois State Troopers! But she took some consolation from the fact she didn't get the gunk assignment because she was a woman and a Jew in a Christian, male-dominated department. She got the dirtiest work because she had the worst possible personal traits in any enterprise: brains and lip. Maybe, someday, somewhere, this combination would be an asset.

But not today.

Today it was just gunk and muck and crud and grime.

Just another dirty assignment.

Rabinowitz punched a button on her sun visor and confirmed receipt of the message. *Here we go*, she mused. *Go out and talk to some Adam Henry with a brain the size of a walnut who had stalled a Winnebago across a railroad track. Great!* This is the kind of assignment you gave a rookie. On the force for more than ten years and still responding to what was one step above a crank call.

There was a locomotive on site, she was told, but it had not struck the Winnebago. The moment the engineer realized there was an obstruction on the track, he had pulled the locomotive to a halt.

She was going to be Code Three until it was confirmed there were no injuries. Then she could cut the siren. But it was going to be the only thrill of the day. The rest of her time was drive and ticket and listen to excuses and then drive and ticket and listen to excuse *ad nausea*. This is what you get for graduating *cum laude* from ESLU, East Saint Louis University? Maybe she should have taken her father's advice and gotten married, But oh, no! She wanted to be a lawyer! There wasn't a dime in the family treasury so here she was, driving a patrol car during the day and taking night classes at the Corodait Law School. Harvard Law it was not but once you passed the Illinois Bar, no one ever asked where you went to school. Then it was all brain and lip. Talk about making lemonade from lemons!

When she pulled up to the Winnebago she found the scene confusing.

Not confused.

Confusing.

What she expected to see were a lot of people milling around a stranded Winnebago saying rude things about someone who was so stupid he got his whale-on-wheels stalled on railroad tracks. How dumb can someone be? The driver could have been a she, of course, but him or her it took a load of brains to get anything stalled on railroad crossing.

But when she arrived at the crossing there was no milling around, no crowd and no angry locomotive engineer stomping up and down in front of the Winnebago having a nose-to-nose discussion with a white-haired matron from somewhere south of the Mason Dixon Line. The metal behemoth was certainly stalled across the rail crossing and a locomotive was stopped less than a hundred yards from the vehicle.

But it was an odd train.

It really wasn't a train at all. It was just a locomotive with a single boxcar behind it. Would you call something that short a train?

Not a soul was milling about the alleged-to-be train or the Winnebago. No one.

There was some road vehicular traffic but it was maneuvering around the Winnebago. When it had become clear the Winnebago was not going to be moving, cars, trucks and busses began driving around it on both sides, the northern-bound traffic on the port side and southern-bound on starboard. The passable road was too narrow for the traffic forcing it to sweep out and around the railroad crossing barrier. The barrier itself had been stopped half-down on the back of the Winnebago, the warning lights were still flashing luridly and sirens were wailing as if they were cursing the obstruction.

If the situation had not been so serious, Rabinowitz would have found it comical. She drove through the center of the bifurcating traffic up to the Winnebago.

The curse of intelligence is it never takes a holiday. Routine is no excuse for turning off your brain. Routine is mankind's greatest shortcoming for it lures us to believe tomorrow will be the same as yesterday. In fact, today is never the same as today. You cannot step in the same river twice, no two mountains are identical and all a girl really wants is for one guy to prove to her all men are not the same. Rabinowitz liked this last quip because it came from Marilyn Monroe, the most underrated star in the Hollywood Pantheon.

The entire scenario before her smelled bad.

The stench wasn't strong enough for her to pull a pistol but she was cautious.

No driver? No engineer berating the driver? No milling crowd? What was going on here? Rather, what was *not* going on here?

She slowed her cruiser as she approached the Winnebago, then changed her mind and reversed gear. Something was clearly amiss. If you do not know what is going on, back away and spend some think time trying to make sense of a nonsensical situation.

So, she backed off.

She pulled a dozen yards back from the railroad crossing and then put the patrol car in park.

But she did not turn the engine off.

Something was very wrong here.

There were no people milling about. Just the train, Winnebago and a smattering of cars cruising around the railroad warning posts on either side of the obstruction. This was not normal. She popped the cruiser into reverse again and slowly started backing away again.

She didn't get very far. Before she had rolled backward a dozen feet a figure dressed in camouflage and carrying an Uzi tapped on her car window. She stopped and the figure indicated she should step out of the car.

She did.

Never argue with someone carrying an Uzi.

CHAPTER 4

Heinz Noonan, the "Bearded Holmes" of the Sandersonville, North Carolina, Police Department was in a life-and-death struggle with a P-38. Noonan liked P-38s though they were getting harder and harder to find. The old ones were the best, the surplus ones. The new ones were simply cheap knockoffs and did not have the strength or longevity of the *real* ones, the military-issue ones. He liked the P-38s because they had a blade as large as he ever needed. Pocket knives were too large and he had lost many a fine one at the TSA counter. Now he no longer bothered to carry pocketknives. A P-38 was just fine because it had enough of a cutting edge to cut string, start the peel on an orange or cut Scotch tape. When the P-38 got dull, he dumped it and pulled another one out of the box in his desk drawer.

This particular P-38 was proving to be a pain in the tulip patch. When he could get it open it had a fine blade. But getting it open was like using a broken key on a sardine can. So here he was, trying to muscle open a P-38, grunting like a sumo wrestler, when incompetence incarnate came into the office.

It was the Sandersonville Commissioner of Homeland Security Edward Paul Lizzard III – (Were there *really* two other Edward Paul Lizzards?)

Here it was, 10 in the a.m. on a Monday and *that man*, Commissioner Lizzard, was going to ruin a perfectly good day of investigating murders, burglaries, bank robberies and kidnapping. What was the world coming to?

Lizzard – who insisted on being called *Commissioner* Lizzard, or simply *Commissioner* –was the embodiment of his reptilian namesake. He was all of five-foot-nothing tall, had the hair of a cue ball and the pallor of chameleon: pasty white when in meetings, mimicking rosacea when he was intent on passing along his problems to anyone else, and sunburn red whenever he spent longer than 30 seconds in sunshine without his trademark Fedora, a hat so old he must have been born with it – and the hat looked it.

Lizzard was a master manipulator of those above him on the administrative food chain. Below him on the same food chain, he was the hot pebble in everyone's shoe. He was constantly committing staff to projects of little value but great political advantage – to himself. He was the only one in the city administration who had glossy business cards – twice the traditionally size and full color – and kept two changes of clothing in his office along with a dozen ties. Why? Because he wanted to "look different" for each of the two television stations in town.

Lizzard had not been a *Commissioner* before 911. Before 911 he had just been Commander Lizzard. Prior he had been Supervisor Lizzard but the title had not been imperial enough for his taste so he convinced the Mayor of Sandersonville – his sister's husband – *Commander* was a more appropriate title. All it would cost was a change in the stationery. His brother-in-law had no wish to upset his own wife so, to keep harmony among collaterals, he agreed to the change.

Then came 911.

Suddenly America was terrorist-crazy and when such hysteria strikes America it is traditionally followed by cash. After every *crash* comes *cash*: c to c from sea to sea. Such is the history of America. Whenever war is declared, be it Iraq, cocaine or illiteracy, the next predictable Congressional milestone is money flowing into the heartland to fix the problem. Lizzard was five steps ahead of the game and had his request for funding from the Office of Homeland Security as the same was being created in Congress. Sandersonville got just enough money for half-a-position, which Lizzard seized. But the caveat was it came with responsibility for staff work which Lizzard happily passed along to his minions in the Sandersonville Police Department Detectives. So, thereafter, unfortunately and too frequently, Lizzard leaned on those minions for tasks, usually meaningless, for which he would claim total credit.

"Good morning, Commissioner," Noonan said falsely. "What can I do for you?"

Lizzard never had time for niceties to those below him on the food chain. "I have just received a missive from Commissioner Mustafa Sanchez in . . "

"Whoa! That's quite a mouthful. A missive? What's a missive?"

"A missive," Lizzard said superciliously, "is a written request. In this case, the *missive*, as you so derogatorily refer to the request, is actually from the combined heads of Homeland Security in Missouri and Illinois."

"There's a joint Homeland Security office for Missouri and Illinois?"

"*Commission*," Lizzard snapped. "Homeland Security *Commission*." Lizzard shook his head as if to clear cranial clutter. "Captain Noonan," he snapped. "This is very serious business. To answer your last question first, no, there is not a special joint Homeland Security Commission for Missouri and Illinois – yet. But since the Mississippi River divides the two, anything affecting traffic crossing or using the river is matter of national security and is considered jointly."

"OK. What did this missive say?

"I don't know."

"You don't know? You got a message and you don't know what it said?"

"No, I got a missive and I understood exactly what it said."

"Well, what did it say?"

"It said our services are needed in East St. Louis immediately."

"East St. Louis? There's such a place? I thought St. Louis was in Missouri."

"It is. But the City of East St. Louis is in Illinois."

"I see. A city with two names divided by a river in two states."

Lizzard thought for a moment. "Yes. That's correct."

"So when the missive said *needed*, does that mean I'm going to East St. Louis?"

"Not just you. You and I."

"Really?" The incredibility of the concept leached out in Noonan's voice. "Anything else I should know?"

"Yes. A passenger train with ten cars and 60 passengers is missing."

"Missing? How can a train go missing?"

"That, *Captain* Noonan," the harsh emphasis on the title *captain* making it clear this was not going to be a buddy-partner assignment, "is what the special joint Homeland Security Commission for Missouri and Illinois wants to know."

CHAPTER 5

Illinois State Trooper Rabinowitz was no stranger to crazy men with guns. After all, she had grown up in a family of crazy men with guns. And women. These were not men and women who hunted. They were just crazy. She was a bit crazy too, she had to admit, but at least she had the good sense to know there were more to life than stockpiling weapons in a working-class neighborhood where everyone drank themselves into an early grave and worried that more and more blacks, Polacks and Muslims were taking their jobs at the factories which had closed two decades earlier. Rabinowitz was used to being around crazy people with guns. A cold sober figure in a ski mask with an Uzi was significantly different.

"Out." That was all that was said. When she stalled, the word was said again. The time the single word was followed by a tapping on her driver's side window with the muzzle of the weapon. It was amazing Rabinowitz thought as she lowered her window, how massive the barrel of a gun looks when it is pointed at you.

"I'd say something funny," she said smiling trying to defuse a tense situation, "but I can't think of anything funny to say."

There was not as much as a flicker of amusement in the eyes half-hidden by the mask.

"Out." There was not a hint as the figure in the ski mask's sex, age or ethnic stock.

"OK, I'm coming."

Rabinowitz slowly reached her right hand across her body to release her seatbelt and ski mask said "Careful." Now the word was long enough to detect this masked, camouflaged figure was female, age indeterminate, ethnic stock unknown.

"I can't get out with the seat belt attached."

"Just move slowly. Bring the car keys with you."

Definitely female now.

Rabinowitz smiled. "It's good to know you can speak in full sentences." If she expected a snappy response, she didn't get it. She popped the seat belt free and then raised both her hands. "Now you have to step back from the door otherwise I cannot get out."

Ski mask didn't say anything. She just stepped back, her Uzi at the ready. Rabinowitz placed her left hand on the top of the patrol car door and waved her right hand. "Now I'm going to pull the keys out of the ignition and open the door with this hand. Let's not do anything foolish."

Ski mask said nothing.

Rabinowitz lowered her hand slowly and pulled on the door handle. The lock popped and she swung the door open. Slowly she put out her left leg and followed it with her right. She stepped out of the patrol car and stood in front of the back tire.

"Now what?"

Ski mask didn't say anything. She just pointed the gun at her belly and gave it a few upward jerks. Rabinowitz looked down and realized ski mask was probably indicating her gun belt.

"You want me to lose my handgun?"

Ski mask didn't say anything, just gestured with the Uzi. The motion was effective.

"I take it you mean 'yes,'" she said. Keeping her left hand up, she dropped her right hand to the gun belt buckle. She slowly unbuckled the belt and let it fall onto the ground. "OK, now what?"

Ski mask didn't say anything. She just jerked the barrel of the Uzi to the left clearly indicating Rabinowitz was to move in that direction.

"You want me to go back toward the Winnebago?"

Ski mask just jerked the Uzi toward the Winnebago.

"I get the message," Rabinowitz said. "It would be a lot easier if you said what you wanted."

Ski mask didn't utter a peep. Rabinowitz didn't either.

Rabinowitz took a half-dozen steps to the left before the ski mask told her to stop but not turn around. Behind her Rabinowitz heard a sound she equated with the ski mask scooping up her gun belt. Then Rabinowitz heard a car door slam – which could only be the patrol car – and the electronic chirp of the door lock.

"Move." Ski mask gave Rabinowitz a jab in the ribs with the Uzi.

They covered the 20 yards quickly and, surprisingly, walked past the stalled Winnebago and progressed down the railway tracks. Surprising as well was the fact no one in any of the cars maneuvering around the stalled, beached whale of a vehicle seemed to notice she was being led away by someone dressed in camouflage wearing a ski mask carrying an Uzi. They probably thought it was part of some movie. Or didn't want to get involved. Either way, no one stopped to offer help. Which was probably a good thing. *Healthy* would have been a better adjective.

Fifteen yards down line Rabinowitz and the ski mask came to the single engine with a boxcar attached. Two other ski masks were waiting.

"A convention?" Rabinowitz refused to give up her sense of humor. "Are we expecting anyone else? Where's the band?"

Surprise Number Three came when one the ski masks spoke in a complete sentence. It was in a cool, collected tone without any hint of a discernable accent. This ski mask was female as well.

"This is serious business, officer. The faster we move, the safer everyone will be. Do you understand?"

"I understand you have kidnapped a law enforcement officer and you are now in very hot water."

"Right now no one is in hot water. At least not yet. Your job right now is to see what is in this boxcar." The woman in the ski mask speaking in complete sentences tapped on the sliding door of the freight car. As she continued to speak, the two other ski masks slid the door back. "Now I need you to report to your office what you see."

Rabinowitz did not have to be a rocket scientist to know what she was looking at. What she saw was an electronic panel with flashing lights, dials and gauge needles. The object, whatever it was, had a slight hum or, more accurately, a dull throb that could have been interpreted as a hum. The panel was flush with the sliding doors of the boxcar.

The ski mask handed her a clipboard with a single sheet of paper and a pen.

"Listen carefully because I will only say this once. This is a block-buster bomb, a remnant of the American arsenal of World War II. You will notice we have put up a sign on the blockbuster: Minor Uncle II. When your office checks with the White Sands, New Mexico testing grounds they will confirm Minor Uncle I was tested on June 10, 1993. It was the last test at White Sands. A second bomb, Minor Uncle II, this one, was never tested. It was mothballed. Now we have it."

The ski mask pulled her closer to the open door of the freight car. "No one is going to believe Minor Uncle II is missing. These numbers are the proof." One of the ski masks pointed to a bank of numbers and letters. "You are to make sure the numbers on the blockbuster match the numbers you are going to write on the sheet of paper." The ski mask indicated a pen she was holding in her hand. Ski mask handed Rabinowitz the pen and a pad of paper. "You will do it now and you will double-check your numbers."

Rabinowitz carefully matched the numbers on the sheet to the numbers on the blockbuster digital pad. It was not as easy as matching 1, 2 and 3 along with A, B and C because there were some symbols she did not recognize. But they all matched.

"Check them again."

"I'm careful. They match. Now what?"

"Check them again anyway. When you call your headquarters, I want you to say you double-checked the numbers. Many lives depend on how you sure you are we are serious and we do have Minor Uncle II."

"If you say so."

"I do."

She checked the numbers and symbols again. "Now what?"

Ski mask nodded his head the other two closed the door to the freight car. "Watch me carefully," ski mask said as he attached a massive electronic lock on the freight car door. Then he turned back to Rabinowitz. "Take out your cell phone."

"What makes you think I have one?"

There was a moment of silence then the ski mask stated flatly, "It will be a whole lot healthier of you lose the lip and cooperate. Cell phone."

Rabinowitz dug around in her pocket and produced her cell phone.

"Shoot a picture of that." Ski mask pointed at the electronic lock. "Your electronic people will recognize it. For your information, this is a fail-safe lock. It can only be opened with a very complicated code. We have the code. After the states of Illinois and Missouri pay us $50 million in diamonds – and only diamonds – we will provide the code to open the electronic lock and disable Minor Uncle II. I must quickly add the lock is booby-trapped – which I am sure your people will know because of the design – to keep anyone from trying to jimmy the lock. If anyone attempts to open this freight car without the code, well, Minor Uncle II goes off. Minor Uncle I had 2,750 short tons of TNT. Minor Uncle II is half the size but still deadly."

"You are going to set off a massive explosion in St. Louis?" For the first time the import of what was happening was becoming clear to Rabinowitz. "You are talking about thousands of dead people!"

"We are aware of that possibility. But we are not heartless. In fact, we'd prefer if this were handled on the QT, as I am sure you can understand."

"You can't just blackmail two states and get away with it!"

"Actually, we can. Here is exactly what we are going to do. But, to your point, we are not heartless. That's why we are going to pull this freight car out onto the Eads Bridge. Under it actually because that's where the railroad tracks run. When the freight car gets to the center of the bridge, directly over the Mississippi River, we are going to uncouple the locomotive and disable this freight car." Ski mask tapped on the freight car for emphasis.

"There are still a lot of people who use the bridge!" Rabinowitz was almost shouting.

Ski mask was calm. "About 8,100 a day according to Wikipedia. The figure does not include trains. But, then again, with the freight car block-ing the rail line no trains will be coming across. We anticipate both Illinois and Missouri will realize it is cheaper to pay us than rebuild the bridge. There is no reason for anyone to be hurt or the bridge to be damaged."

"And you are telling me this because. . ." Rabinowitz let the sentence hang.

"Because you are going to take a trip with us. You and the three of us are going to take the boxcar out to the center of the Eads Bridge. You will watch as we disable the freight car and then, fair lady, you will walk back to your patrol car and report everything I have said."

"What are you going to do?"

"I and my colleagues will be on the locomotive. We will ride into East St. Louis, abandon the locomotive and we shall disappear into the landscape."

"Then how are you going to get your diamonds?"

"Someone will arrive at the East St. Louis City Hall. He will handle the transaction."

"Someone? Does this person have a name?"

"George."

"Just George. No last name?"

"Please, officer. Let's treat each other as intelligent human beings. Just George. He will arrive, check the stones for authenticity. When he is satisfied, the total amount has been reached and no cosmetic stones have been included, he will give you the code to disable the bomb."

"What makes you think we will trust you to keep your end of the bargain?"

"You don't. But then again we don't trust you. We both have to take it on faith the other person will live up to the bargain."

"A devil's bargain."

It was possible to see the fabric around the ski raise a little indicating the lips beneath made a smile. "I am in the devil's business, dear lady."

"You won't get away with this."

"Wanna bet?" Ski mask indicated the direction of the locomotive with a lift of an Uzi. As Rabinowitz started to walk away, ski mask stopped her with a hand on her shoulder.

"One more thing. We anticipate there will be some, shall we say, reluctance on the part of the state governments to deal with the realities. They just might stall and stall and stall. This is why Minor Uncle II also has a timed fuse. Forty-eight hours from now Minor Uncle II will go off. "

Ski mask dropped Rabinowitz's patrol car keys in her hand. "The clock is ticking, officer, the clock is ticking. Now, let's take a train ride."

CHAPTER 6

The drive from Sandersonville to Virginia Beach was absolute agony for Chief of Detectives Heinz Noonan. It was not as if the roadway had been chopped up into construction sections – which it was neither (chopped up nor contained construction sections) – or weather hampered their progress. This was not the case either. What *was* the case was the ongoing, tedious, mundane soliloquy of Commissioner Lizzard of his more important cases – all one of them – which he related to Noonan in unending excruciating detail.

Numerous times.

In a running commentary, which began as soon as Noonan slid behind the wheel of the unmarked and Lizzard clambered into the dead man's seat. Then, for the next four hours, Lizzard droned on and on and on and on and on and on and on and on only offering Noonan just enough time to mumble such comments as "uh-huh," "hum" and "mmmm" with the lowest level of enthusiasm the detective could vocally muster. The only bit of meaningful information Lizzard provided Noonan was his, Lizzard's, aunt, lived in St. Louis and "this adventure," as Lizzard called it, "was the perfect opportunity to mix business with pleasure." Lizzard did not add the magic words: "all paid for by the Office of Homeland Security."

In the rare moments when Lizzard was not discussing his most important case, he was on his cell phone with St. Louis, Missouri Commissioner Mustafa Sanchez who was now the Acting Head of Operations – "HO" as Lizzard kept calling him – of the combined heads of Homeland Security in Missouri and Illinois. Noonan listened to Lizzard's end of the conversation with reluctant interest. Lizzard and Sanchez were peas in a pod and the heavy stench of politics filled the sedan.

An hour out of Virginia Beach things got serious. With no explanation offered, Noonan and Lizzard were given directions to a landing strip with no name. It had never had a name. This was not because it was a secret Homeland Security operational base but because it was nothing more than a broad stretch of an abandoned roadway occasionally used by crop dusters. The two men were told to remain on the side of the landing strip to "await instructions." Noonan, scratching his head and rolling his eyes, complied with the "instructions" while Lizzard was giddy with excitement over the possibility something hush-hush was going on where he would be personally involved. He was already field-testing his statement to the press as Noonan headed for the landing strip.

Lizzard did not know how right he was.

On the so-called landing strip was a helicopter – black, of course. Noonan and Lizzard were hustled aboard for their flight to East St. Louis. Yelling above the roar of the rotor blade, a man in the uniform of an Illinois State Trooper pulled the two men aboard. There were only three seats in the chopper, one for the pilot and one of the others was filled with a man of about 20. The young man got off the chopper and only stopped long enough to take the car keys from Noonan's hand. The young man said something which Noonan could not hear above the roar of the rotor blades. Noonan assumed it was the unmarked would be delivered back to Sandersonville. Noonan was about to suggest to Lizzard he, Noonan, ought to go back to Sandersonville with the car. He never got the chance. Before he could be seated in the chopper the pilot handed Noonan a set of headphones and indicated he should put them on. When Lizzard indicated he should have a headset as well, the pilot indicated either there was only one headset available or the communication was for Noonan only. In either case, Lizzard was in a huff.

Noonan was not broken-hearted.

"Captain Noonan," a voice crackled over the head set. "You come highly recommended."

"For what?"

"I wish we had time for niceties," the voice continued. "But the situation has changed substantially in the last two hours. We need your expertise immediately. That's why we sent the helicopter."

"It's a long way from Virginia Beach to St. Louis," Noonan yelled into the mouthpiece. "Can this helicopter make it all the way to St. Louis?"

"Not a chance," the voice came back, "You're only going as far as the Virginia Beach airport. Then you are going by Lear jet."

"That's not going to save much time."

"Every second counts."

"OK. Tell me what you've got."

"You won't believe it. Do you have a pen and paper?"

"No, but I'm a memory expert."

"That's a Don Adams line."

Noonan was pleased someone remembered Don Adams. "More likely Buck Henry. Whatcha got?"

"Sixteen hours ago, yesterday afternoon 60 travel writers disappeared somewhere between St. Louis and Chicago."

Noonan strained to hear. Then he said, "Disappeared as in they were on a plane which dropped off the radar or were sucked into the rings of Saturn off the street?"

"Neither. They were on a train."

"As in the Little Engine that could?"

"Yes. It was a FAM trip. Do you know what a FAM is?"

"Not really."

"FAM stands for 'familiarization.' In this case, it means getting 60 travel writers together and taking them on a three-day weekend holiday to Chicago and showing them just how great it would be for their readers to visit Chicago."

"So, it's junket for them."

"Essentially, yes. All they could eat and drink at the best hotels and all they had to do was write a nice story about Chicago and the trains which can get you there."

"Let me guess. Those travel writers who play the game get to go to Chicago again next year."

"You understand the game perfectly, captain."

"Heinz."

"Eh?'

"Heinz. I'm not a captain in Illinois."

"I'm not a captain in Illinois either. I'm Archie Yenokovian. Just call me Archie."

"Of Homeland Security?"

"No. I'm with the Illinois State Troopers. Mustafa Sanchez is the Commissioner of Homeland Security."

"I hate to ask. What is the chain of command there in St. Louis?"

"Well, if it were just the train, I'd be your contact. But with the bomb on the bridge, no one really knows. That's why the joint Homeland Security Commission for Missouri and Illinois was formed."

"Bomb?"

"When it rains it pours. That's the urgency now. You and I now work for Homeland Security."

"Ah," said Noonan, "the stench of politics."

"You've been reading my mail," replied Archie.

CHAPTER 7

The closest James Elroy Whittaker had ever come to an Uzi was in a movie theater. He knew what the weapon was, of course. Everyone does. Everyone also knows it can be a very nasty weapon at the business end. So, when the two figures with the ski mask came into the cab of the locomotive, Whittaker knew his day was going to change for the worse.

He was correct.

In less than ten seconds the ski masks shut off the GPS monitors in the dome cars and locomotive. As Whittaker was being flex cuffed and hustled out of the locomotive cab he could hear the **Bonanza** Command & Control, C&C, squawking over the communication system it had lost the train on the railway grid.

CHAPTER 8

I s this some kind of a blond joke?"

That was the response coming over the cellphone when Rabinowitz reported the bomb on the Eads Bridge. Let's hear it for sexual equality in the workplace, she thought. Rabinowitz was not even blond. At least she had hair. The man at the other end of the cell phone call, her sergeant, three years older than she was, had started shaving his head because he was losing what hair he had once had.

"Negative," she had repeated into the cell phone as she stumbled on the railroad cross beams walking back toward the stalled Winnebago.

Before she could add anything, her sergeant snapped angrily, "Why are you on a cell phone?"

"Because I'm walking back along the railway ties to the patrol car. Even if I were in the patrol car I'd be using the cell. The press monitors the police band. This is not something we want out and around."

It galled her to say *sir.*

So she didn't.

If it bothered the Neanderthal on the other end of the electronic beam, he didn't say so.

The man was still skeptical. "We've got a bunch of yahoos who want $50 million in diamonds or they're gonna blow up a bridge?!"

"That's what they said."

"Get back to the patrol car, Rabinowitz, and stay there!" The voice had a sharp edge to it. "I'll get back with you."

Before she could respond the call went dead.

"Well," she said to herself, "goodbye and thank you for being diligent, patrolwoman. Not at all, Sarge, not at all."

CHAPTER 9

I t would have been easy to call the railroad warehouse at the foot of the Eads Bridge a beehive of activity. But such a description would have been incorrect. While a beehive is busy – the cliché "busy as a beehive" being appropriate – every bee in a swarm has an innate understanding of its role, function and purpose. The hive is organized and there is no superfluous activity. The bees, individually and collectively, know exactly what they are doing.

This was not the case in the warehouse.

The only thing organized about the warehouse was the list of people to be allowed in. Noonan had to show his badge and identification twice before he could enter the structure while Lizzard simply nodded to a man standing next to the guard. Such was all that was needed for his Excellency. Whether Lizzard's name was on the list or not was not known to Noonan. All Noonan did know was he, Noonan, had to leap through bureaucratic hoops to get into a game he had been ordered to play while Lizzard simply waltzed through the double front doors as if he were royalty.

In fact, he was.

He had a connection with the Commissioner of Homeland Security for East St. Louis and a royal connection was all that was necessary to get into the beehive. No one checked to see if Noonan was armed – he was not – while Lizzard was always armed with a deadly weapon: his tongue.

Command centers like this were old hat to Noonan. Once into the inner chamber the room was divided into two types of people. Those who did the work and those who took the credit; the people of sweat and the people of show. They were all intermingling in the room but it did not take Noonan long to break them apart. It was simple. It was a process of elimination. All he had to do was keep track of the people Lizzard was glad-handing and backslapping. These were the people of show.

That left less than half a dozen.

Which Noonan identified in a glance.

It was easy.

They were working.

A man tall enough to play basketball – and probably had – came over and extended a scarecrow-like arm. He was dressed in the uniform of the Illinois State Troopers. He might have been all of 30.

"Archibald Yenokovian. We talked on the phone. The 'v' is silent."

"What 'v?'"

"The 'v' in my last name. The one no one can spell. Just call me Archie. Everyone does."

"Great. I'm Heinz. That's what everyone calls me unless I'm in trouble. Then I'm CAPTAIN!"

Archie smiled. "We'll get along just fine. If the situation were normal we'd have a little friendly chat but we are up against one nasty crew. I'm glad you're here and can hit the ground running."

"What's the situation as we speak?"

"Odd, I must tell you. First, we have a short train composed of a locomotive, dining car and three dome cars that have disappeared. There are 60 travel writers on the train, a crew of 10 including the engineer."

"What do you mean 'disappeared?'"

"They dropped of the electronic grid. Almost every piece of railroad rolling stock has GPS capabilities. It's the GPS that allows railroad owners to keep track of all their rolling stock. Even though there are about 140,000 miles of track in the United States, every railroad company knows where every one of its cars is at any moment."

"Even the old cars?"

"Good point. Yes and no. Yes, the companies know where each car is if the car has an operating GPS. No, the older cars – many of them anyway – don't have GPS. The rail cars without GPS could be too old to be used and are on a siding or have the GPS turned off to save money."

"How about the rail cars that are missing? Didn't they have GPS."

"They all have GPS capabilities but they went ghost. At 2:27 Friday afternoon. All the GPS on all the three dome cars, locomotive and dining car went ghost."

"Isn't that unusual? I mean, all of them going out at the same time."

"Yes. Which is why we're sure all the GPS monitors were turned off. They were working fine in the a.m. Friday morning and suddenly went blank. All within minutes of each other. The company tried to raise the conductor on the radio and on a cell phone but got zip."

"I'm guessing you can turn the GPS off from the locomotive."

"Another yes and no answer. Yes, it can be done but it's not as easy as hitting a switch. You have to know what you are doing. But it can be done. No, it's not possible to have all the GPS monitors go ghost at the same time because of an electronic malfunction. They have to be individually shut off manually."

"Cell phones? I'm assuming at least some of the 70 people on board had phones. Didn't any of them work?"

"Ghost too. As if they never existed. We lost contact with the engineer at 2:27 and by three it was clear something was very wrong. The railroad company contacted the police who contacted the Illinois State Troopers." Archie pointed to his badge.

"Why the Illinois State Troopers? You are responsible for the highways, not rail lines."

"That's because of the Winnebago. All part of the same scenario."

"Winnebago? That's news to me. But let's finish with the train first," Noonan said. "At 2:27 p.m. the GPS goes ghost – I like the term, by the way. Then the railway company cannot raise the engineer on the locomotive communication system or on his personal cell phone."

"Correct."

"I'm assuming the communication system works even if the train is in a tunnel."

"You are correct again. The railway communication network is wireless, of course, and works just like a cell phone. Cell phones work in tunnels."

"I know this is very a silly question, but is there a master map showing where all of the trains on the railways system are at any one moment?"

"You are just racking up the 'yes and no' answers today. No, there is no master map – your term – for the whole United States or any state. There are electronic grids for metropolitan areas. This particular train was running north to Chicago. It was on the St. Louis grid but as soon as it left the metropolitan area it was only being tracked by satellite. *Tracking* is bad term to use because the satellite was not focusing on the train. It was simply recording electronic information from all box-cars, locomotives and rolling stock on all lines within the scope of its coverage. It was not as if the satellite is tracking any one specific train. Then, as soon as the train gets close to Chicago it would pop up on the Chicago grid. It never got close. There's a lot of farm country between St. Louis and Chicago. The train left the St. Louis grid and never popped onto the Chicago grid."

"I'm guessing the train cannot be on the main track otherwise it would have been spotted."

"You are really getting a passel of 'yes and no' answers today. Yes, if the train were on a frequently used line it would have been spotted. But there are hundreds of miles of spur track and railyards along the way. It's a short train and it could have pulled off onto a siding and be hiding in plain sight."

"How about satellite pictures? Doesn't the military have razzle dazzle downward looking radar?"

"Yes, but spotting an individual train will take time. If the military decided to help it could go back over its tapes – assuming it uses tapes – and find the train as it was leaving the St. Louis grid. Then it could follow it until it disappeared. But it will take time to get the tapes and the satellite pictures have a very narrow window. We might spot the train as it was moving and then the satellite would be out of range as the train was still moving."

"It won't do much good to send a drone to look for the train, I'm guessing."

"We asked and the Air Force complied. But you're right, it's not going to do too much good. There are hundreds of miles of siding and all kinds of rail cars sitting idle. Besides, visually, looking down at a dome car does not tell you anything except it's a dome car. Without a

GPS squawking an overflight cannot tell if a locomotive is the missing one or one with the GPS turned off. Eventually we'll find the train. It's just a matter of time."

"And we don't have time."

"That's right. Forty-eight hours and the clock is ticking. We've got a bomb with a 48-hour fuse. Which is why you were spirited in on a chopper."

"There's a timetable?"

"A bomb involved as well."

"Let's finish with the train first. Since the train went ghost there hasn't been a peep."

"Not one."

"You know the passengers are going to be part of the mix?" Noonan gave a concerned look. "We are talking about lives here, not just a missing train."

"We do not know if the two events are connected. Not yet, anyway. We have a missing train with 70 people on board. We also have a handful of perpetrators who have placed a large bomb on the Eads Bridge over the Mississippi. They want $50 million in diamonds."

"Now let's talk about the bomb."

Archie changed gears effortlessly. "This afternoon the Illinois State Troopers responded to an alert. A Winnebago was stalled on the railroad tracks on the Missouri side of the Mississippi. A patrolwoman responded and was taken temporary prisoner."

"Temporary?"

"Yes. She was only held for a very short time. At that time, she was shown a large bomb in a boxcar and told to write down the serial number for the bomb. She did and we have confirmed the serial numbers match a bomb missing from a federal bomb storage facility in New Mexico. She also reported, with a cell phone picture I might add, the boxcar door is booby-trapped with an electronic lock. She was then released and as she was walking back to her vehicle, the boxcar with the bomb was pulled out onto the Eads Bridge," he stalled for a moment. "Which is the bridge over the Mississippi routing traffic into East St. Louis."

"So the bomb is on the bridge?"

"As we speak, yes. Inside of it, actually. The railroad tracks run beneath the car and truck traffic. The patrolwoman was told the perps want $50 million in diamonds or they would blow the bridge. We are supposed to start gathering – in fact, we are gathering – diamonds and are to deliver them to a man named George who is going to make an appearance."

"When?"

"We don't know."

"Where?"

"We don't know. All we know is we have an active bomb on a bridge and until we can come up with an alternate plan, we have to gather the diamonds and pay the ransom."

"Is there any connection between the missing dome cars and the bomb?"

"We don't know. We assume they are related but, at this moment, no, we have nothing solid to link the two."

"If they are connected," Noonan said scratching his beard. "Why kidnap 70 people? It doubles your chance of being caught."

"I agree. It's odd. But if the two events are connected the bad people have planned well in advance. They know what they are doing."

As Noonan was thinking Archie cut in. "And before you ask, yes, we are looking for the inside people. No one call pull off a railway disappearing act like this unless they have inside knowledge."

"And before you say it," Noonan smiled. "I'm guessing you are going to tell me it is going to take time to find the person and it is unlikely you'll be able to turn over every rock within 48 hours."

"Correct. We'll be able to piece the entire caper together eventually. But we've got to pay the diamonds within 48 hours. The passengers are our priority."

"Not the bridge."

"Not the bridge. Bridge's cannot sue."

CHAPTER 10

Alaskan humorist Warren Sitka once noted when hyenas meet in congress, the jungle trembles. While anyone can debate the double meaning of *congress*, no one doubts the sagacity of the adage.

Homeland Security Commissioner for Sandersonville, North Carolina, Edward Paul Lizzard III was huddled with St. Louis Homeland Security Commissioner Mustafa Sanchez when they were joined by East St. Louis Homeland Security Commissioner Boris Yang. The assembled commissioners were, to overuse a cliché, peas in a pod. Mixing metaphors, they made no bones about it. To them the disappearing dome train, bomb in the Eads Bridge and extortion of both cities of St. Louis – and the states of Missouri and Illinois – for $50 million was not a crisis. It was a cause for celebration! It was an unexpected bonanza, an opportunity not to be missed. They saw headlines!

It was a twin crisis with no downside for only three men: Lizzard, Sanchez and Wang. What happened to the missing travel writer and train crew – when they were found – was going to be in the hands of hostage negotiators who had no connection with the commissioners. BUT – and the commissioners were quick to seize upon the *but* – the abductions had occurred on a federally-regulated rail line which made it a federal offense and thus allowed the commissioners a nose of the camel under the tent. Further, all three commissioners were clock-watching courtesy of the Little Lindberg Law. Once 24 hours had passed – as per the Federal Kidnapping Act – it would be assumed the kidnappers had crossed a state line. Even if they had not, the kidnapping would be a federal offense. At 24 hours and one second, the last vestige of any state's responsibility would evaporate leaving the situation solely a federal matter and they – a federally-recognized triumvirate would be allowed more than the proverbial nose of the camel under the tent. Best of all, at one second after the 24-hours expired, the joint commissioners could claim a share of authority – *but no responsibility* – for the ongoing efforts which, a blessing to them, they would have no hand in investigating but would be the mouthpiece for the press.

As to the *alleged* bomb, again, the commissioners were triple blessed. First, there was no rock-solid proof there was a bomb at all. The minions of the United States government could only say definitively that no one could find Minor Uncle II. This did not necessarily mean there ever was a Minor Uncle II. Yes, there was federal paperwork on Minor Uncle II, but that was the extent of it. It was not as if there was a shelf and the Minor Uncle II shelf-space was empty. Minor Uncle II could have been just the figment of some paper-ushers' imagination or, equally as likely, a paperwork scheme to get more money from the Department of Defense during the Cold War. Whether or not Minor Uncle II ever did exit was not the point. The point was the threat of an explosion of a large bomb was real. Since the threat was real, the commissioners could claim caution even though they were absolutely, positively sure there was no such need.

Second, the *alleged-to-be* bomb was the sole responsibility of the United States Department of Defense because the bomb – if it existed at all – was, in the final analysis, federal property. Yes, yes, yes, the combined bomb squads of the two St. Louis law enforcement entities and the two-state law enforcement agencies were on duty – but only as backup. The Department of Defense may have been the lead in this operation but it was gargantuan and not coordinated on the ground in East St. Louis. But the joint commission was coordinated. The commissioners had moved fast and seized the microphone, as it were. They were now the go-to source of information for the press.

Third, and least important, the $50 million in diamonds was simply a dollop of red ink on some governmental spreadsheet inevitably to turn to black when the city attorneys – double the word *city* and multiply the word *attorneys* – took the double cities, double states, multiple insurance companies and single United States government to court to recoup the cost of the purloined diamonds.

The bottom line: there was no downside for the joint commissioners.

It had taken the three commissioners less than a nanosecond to realize they were in a unique bureaucratic position: in the catbird seat. You couldn't get any better than this. They could demand immediate, emergency funding to oversee a crisis they would have no hand in resolving but, at the same time would have to "monitor carefully." This would require staff. Staff for which none of the offices had funding. Further, as the bomb was in and on a bridge which spanned the Mississippi River, the negative impact of an explosion would affect two states as well as the "navigable integrity of the most expansive waterway in the continental United States." The exact wording of the request for more funding was created by Wang, approved by Sanchez and sent by Lizzard who had "a close relative" in the upper reaches of the bowels of Homeland Security in Washington D. C.

It was who you *knew* that counted; not what you *know* – or, in the case of Homeland Security, how competent you were.

CHAPTER 11

There are many places in the world where reality does not exist. As an example, if you live along the coastline in the Arctic you accept a *polynya* as a fact of life even though it cannot be explained and, from a scientific point of view, is impossible. A *polynya* is an open spread of seawater surrounded by ice five to ten feet thick. From October to May the surface of the Bering Sea is covered with ten feet of ice. But the ice is not solid from Alaska to Siberia. In places, there are open bodies of water, called *polynyas*, which defy scientific explanation. Why, when the temperature is 40 degrees below zero, are there lakes of exposed water surrounded by ice ten feet thick?

There are other places on earth where there are flaws in reality. While it is certainly true one and one equals two and to dig a hole you must go into the earth, but these are only realities in the real world. This is because there is general agreement these realities are universal. One and one equals two in Egypt, on the moon and in every elementary school second grade class. But one and one does *not* equal two anywhere along either bank of the Potomac River within the 68.34 square miles – 177 square kilometers – which comprise what the world knows as Washington D. C. This is not because of a glitch in the space-time continuum or some aberration in the celestial order of all things. It is because it is Washington D. C., a city where the answer is derived before the question. Thus, logic is reversed. One can never dig a budgetary hole because it is being filled faster than it is progressing downward. So the alleged hole is actually going in the reverse direction. It is a land where one and one equals what the accountants want it to be.

Second Undersecretary to the Commissioner of Homeland Security was at his usual, unusual meeting with his compeers from Justice and Defense. It was a usual meeting because it occurred every Thursday at 2 in the afternoon. It was unusual because the site of the meeting changed weekly. Today it was in Lafayette Park, a bold move because it was within eyeshot of the White House. But then again, it was not unusual because it was an election year and the woman in the White House was Republican.

Which is why the three of them had their jobs.

It was also in their interest to keep that woman in the White House because all three were a handful of years from retirement. No reason to scramble in the weeds for another measly four years.

The events in both cities of St. Louis was common knowledge among the insiders in Washington D. C. But it was ho-hum knowledge. None of the security gurus were on the ground in either St. Louis cities. This meant everything was done via minions. Communication up and down the administrative food chain was rapid but incomplete.

When the matter came to their collective attention, each one did what was generic – and required – in similar circumstances: the minimum.

Not that there were any other similar circumstances.

Defense authorized the nearest Special Forces contingent at Fort Leonard Wood to provide snipers and electronic surveillance as well as drone overflights. Justice authorized a retired agent to be placed back on active duty to "advise" local law enforcement. Homeland Security funneled all orders, information and assessments through the three on-the-ground commissioners in East St. Louis. The fact there was an extra commissioner did not bother Justice, Defense or Homeland Security. It was just one more person in the mix. The more cooks there were, the greater the chances of confusion and if there was any one thing Justice, Defense and Homeland Security wanted it was chaos. For in chaos there was profit. This matter did not look serious but, with elegance, it could be misconstrued into being a terrorist act.

Nothing was better for an incumbent President than peacefully – and publicly – resolving a terrorist episode.

It was an autonomic response to a minuscule matter of national importance: Level One Threat.

When a Level One Threat was encountered, the initial response was the same. It was announced and followed quickly with a press conference and news release. It was, in street parlance, a bluff. Snipers were ordered on alert and overflights were ordered. But the snipers rarely left a base and overflights were unmanned which meant no pilots left the barracks. At the end of the day it was a huge plus for public relations and not a dime of expenditure on personnel.

It was routine: SNAFU and the public ate it up.

The three conspirators only needed a brief window of opportunity.

The election was six months out and every day talking of readiness was one more day of the President looking tough on terrorism without spending a dime.

The good news traveled down the administrative food chain. What was good for the President was good for Justice.

And Defense

And Homeland Security.

All they needed was a lot of publicity and a delicious ending.

They had the staff on the ground.

A faux crisis.

How could they fail?

CHAPTER 12

I t was quite an experience for sure. It was so strange Whittaker was still trying to put the pieces of the jigsaw puzzle together even as events were transpiring. Zip tied in the dining car immediately behind the locomotive he was helpless to do anything but feel the locomotive as it slowed almost to a stop and then took a side spur off the main line. He knew something was afoot but he was sure none of the passengers knew they were being hijacked. After all, they were in the dome cars. They had absolutely no idea what to expect from the train ride. Whatever happened was normal. If the train slowed, it slowed. It was no big deal. In fact, it was no deal at all. If the train was forced to take a spur run, so be it. So what if the train was late? There was plenty of liquor in the dome cars – free, it should be added. There was more than enough food for three days; no one was complaining. Hey, this trip could last until next Thursday as far as anyone board was concerned. Just as long as the toilets didn't plug what was there to worry about?

The good times in the dome cars ended when the train came to a full stop and a handful of individuals dressed in camouflage with ski masks covering their faces came on board. Six of them, two per dome car. One at a time the passengers were wanded and sent out the dome car doors and into one of two buses. No computers, no cell phones, no luggage and empty pockets. 60 passengers and ten crew members. Whittaker was the last to be wanded and loaded aboard the last bus. As the buses headed out in a cloud of dust, Whittaker watched as the locomotive with the now-empty dome cars began to shuttle along the spur line.

CHAPTER 13

Rabinowitz was sitting exactly where she had been ordered to sit: on the front seat of her patrol car. She was in the eye of an expanding hurricane of activity and the only one in the calm. There was no reason for her to be *in situ*. Actually, there was. She was *persona non-grata* in her department. So, it left her to sit.

As she sat, the Winnebago was driven off to the Missouri Crime Laboratory. 100% of the documentation of the bomb had been sent via the FBI to wherever such information is sent. The East St. Louis police department had taken control of the abandoned locomotive on the eastern side of the Mississippi. Here she was, sitting on the front seat of her patrol car, waiting for instructions.

Two hours later she was still sitting there.

What could possibly happen on this stretch of abandoned railway tracks?

When she asked why she was still in her patrol car, all she was told was "it will keep you out of trouble." This statement wasn't sexual harassment. It was flat-out, legal harassment destined to make you want to go away and find a job somewhere else. It wasn't a hint; it was as close to an order as you could legally get.

CHAPTER 14

James Elroy Whittaker had absolutely no idea where he and the other hostages were. There was no reason he should have known. Or could have known. As an engineer he was never required to know where he was and thus maps in the conventional sense of the term were superfluous sheets of paper. He was the captain of a steel vessel on tracks that offered no choice of route. He "rode the rails" in the 21st Century version of the term. Where they were, he went.

More important, distance was not a function of geography but time and track conditions. He was managed by his schedule. Weather had no bearing on his journey, only cows, curves and crossings. Distance in the conventional sense of the term was simply the number of minutes and seconds north, south, east or west of the next rail intersection. The only sense of time being variable in his life was when a mile was 5, 280 feet in length and he was driving his automobile. Even then, only then if he were not on the interstate. If he were on the interstate, the 5,280 feet was 60 seconds at 60 miles per hour.

Seated on the bus he was in rare circumstance. He was traveling in a vehicle in which he was not in control. He was a passenger and in one of two buses, all packed with unruly, frightened, swearing individuals, many of them inebriated on either their own verbosity or the complimentary champagne courtesy of the Bonanza Travel Agency, the host of the FAM.

The journey had not been long, a half-hour at the longest. Then the buses, in queue, had pulled off the highway and plunged into the countryside. After several miles of what could only be described as country roads – with the accent on country— the buses made a sharp turn and sliced their way through a veneer of thick shrubbery. On the far side of the hedgerow was a wide-open field. It was odd this field was fallow and not with corn as high as an elephant's eye. Sixty yards later the buses took a hard right and then, for the first time, everyone on the buses could see their destination out of the port side windows.

Whatever it had once been, it was now abandoned. That was clear from the condition of the structures. What had once been a cheery blue and white was now a depressing brown and grey with water streaks down the sides of the buildings. Weeds had woven their way up through the cyclone fence and a sea of thigh-high shrubs engulfed the squat buildings. There were patches of chest-high thickets here and there and, most ominously, the entire compound was encircled with a double ring of ten-foot high cyclone fences topped with razor wire. The razor wire was rusted but nonetheless achieved the reverse purpose for which it was installed – in this case, keeping people in, not out.

Seated toward the back of the second bus, Whittaker could not see what was transpiring ahead of the first bus. All he knew for certain was the twin buses did not stop at either the front gate to the compound or the second, security gate 30 feet back. He saw no one opening any gate – or gates. Both buses just whizzed through the double helix of cyclone fences topped with razor wire. From his side of the bus he saw no one as the buses passed into the compound. If the gates closed behind the second bus – his bus – he had no way of knowing.

He was on his own.

Everyone was.

Everyone knew it.

It had not been a pleasant afternoon. They had been wanded and searched before being stampeded into the two buses. There had been no effort to make them comfortable. Half of them went into the first bus and the second half in the second. There were six people sitting on the floor in Whittaker's bus and probably about as many on the floor of the other bus as well. The windows were welded shut and tinted dark. No one on the outside could see anyone inside signaling for help.

If there had been anyone on the outside to look in.

There had not been.

From the train to the compound it had been backcountry roads with nothing moving but the dust billows behind the bus convoy.

There had been a lot of yelling at the driver but to no avail. He – or it could have been a *she* – was locked inside a metal box at the front of the bus. When the yelling started, canned music started. When the yelling got louder, the canned music became louder. Banging on the windows did not shatter them – though several the hostages tried – and there were no fire extinguishers or other safety equipment which could be pulled from their bracings and used to break the windows. They were stuck inside where it was hot, muggy and replete with curses and expressions of fear that this story was not going to have a happy ending.

Whittaker's bus came to a stop bumper-to-bumper with the first bus beside a dilapidated two-story structure. As they sat waiting – for the first time since they had come aboard the bus – a tinny voice came over the intercom. It was asexual. Everyone was told to remain calm. The first bus was being evacuated. When their turn came, they were to exit the bus and enter the building. There was no reason for anyone to be heroic. Just enter the building. Anyone left behind hiding in the bus would be shot.

That was all that was said.

When the first bus was empty, it pulled away. Whittaker's bus took its place and everyone walked off the bus, single file into the building. Whittaker saw no one in the sliver of daylight between the bus door and the building door. When everyone was inside, both doors closed behind them — bus and building. Then Whittaker heard the building door being locked behind him followed the sound of receding engines as the buses drive away.

It had taken the hostages less than half a heartbeat to fully assess where they were. The instant some of the more ambitious writers were inside the structure they ran for the exits. But the exit doors were barred from the inside with two-by-fours. These were minor obstacles. It did not take long for the combined strength of a dozen men to rip the two-by-four beams from the doorframes. Then it was out of the building and into the compound yard.

By then the buses were gone.

Once outside no one got far because there was nowhere to go.

Yes, there were three exit points around the fenced circumference but all were chained shut – including the one used by the bus convoy. Then the hostages broke into the other half-dozen structures looking for a phone but to no avail.

Everyone finally regrouped in the initial structure where the buses had abandoned them.

"OK," someone yelled. Whittaker didn't know who it was, just someone who wanted to be in charge. "We're here. What next?"

"Well," another voice chimed in. "At least we've got food and the faucet works."

"Let's hope the toilets work too." This was followed by a chorus of *hear-hear.*

There were some half-hearted, snippy statements. Whittaker decided someone should be in charge. Since no one was taking charge, he did.

"I'm James Whittaker. I'm the engineer."

"*Were* the engineer," someone said.

"I *was* the engineer, correct. I *was* the engineer. Right now, we've got to get organized because we are alone. I don't know what has happened. All I know is we are stuck here for the moment. There is going to be a search for us. Starting right now we need to do everything we can to make it as easy as possible for someone, anyone to find us."

"And how do we do that?" It was the same voice as before, this time oozing with irony.

"Well, to start, I suggest we start a fire. This place is abandoned and if someone sees a fire they will report it. At least it's a start. Then I suggest we find things we can use to reflect sunlight. We should have a few of us on the roofs flashing lights in all directions. Someone is going to see the flashes and call the police."

"You seem awfully sure of yourself," someone said.

"Not at all," Whittaker replied. "All I can say for sure is we are going to be found. Whatever game those hijackers are playing, we are very small pieces in their very large chess game."

"How do you know that," snapped someone else.

"Because we are here alone. There is no one watching us. It's probably because the hijackers figure we'll be found within a day or two. That's probably just enough time for them to pull off whatever scheme they have planned. No, we're out of their field of play. What we have to do now is screw up their schedule."

"So we have to be found early."

"Yup," replied Whittaker. "As early as possible. We must screw up their time schedule. The single advantage we have is everyone is going to be out looking for us. The minute we don't show up on time the railroad monitors will call the police. They must. It's police procedure. A half-later there will be a thousand pairs of eyes looking for us. We need to make ourselves as visible as possible."

"Sounds reasonable," someone said. "I'm a smoker. I've still got my lighter. See if we can find some paper or kindling to start a fire."

As the crowd started to break apart, a woman yelled, "Let's see if can find some pots or pans to flash SOS!"

CHAPTER 15

Archie and Noonan were huddled around the Formica table which had been jammed against a distant wall of the warehouse. Both men referred to the wall as "distant" because it was "distant" from the hubbub of the politically-inclined crowd. That crowd, dominated by the three Homeland Security alleged-to-be professionals, was being sent hither and yon on all manner of assignments. The most pressing of assignments was the accumulation of the $50 million in diamonds

The gathering of the diamonds was odd for number of reasons. First, no one knew what they were doing in the sense that the diamonds were not evidence. *Evidence* was a legally defined item for which law enforcement in every community in America from backwater to metropolitan had a procedure. Thus, there was as a chain of provenance for these beat cops. But the diamonds were not evidence. They were just cargo. There were no procedures for picking up valuable cargo and thus there was chaos. Even though the twin cities of St. Louis, backed by the governors' offices of both states, had agreed to stick the bills for the diamonds on the insurance companies – whomever they may be – there were still the mechanics of collecting the stones. No jeweler was just going to hand over diamonds to someone dressed like a cop. Anyone can dress like a cop. Anyone can call the jewelry store and say they were with the Governor's office and explain they needed diamonds. There were procedures, you know. But no one knew what those procedures were – because they did not exist.

Slowing the process considerably, about sixty insurance companies had to be contacted and, one at a time, they had to contact individual jewelers and assure them, individually, the stones would be covered by insurance. This would have not been a difficult task if it were not for such impediments as nightfall, suspicious administrative assistants who would call the police when such calls came in, reaching jewelry store owners on vacation, maneuvering around current disputes between jewelry store owners and their insurance companies, jewelry stores with multiple insurance companies and jewelry stores behind on their insurance payments. Then there was the problem of sending cops out to collect the jewels in groups because – though unsaid – it would not be to have a stone or two "fall out of an envelope onto the floorboards" and not be found until later.

If ever.

Then, as the stones came into the warehouse, they had to be matched against the inventory sheets from the insurance companies.

Twice.

Again, unspoken, this was said to be for "security reasons" which, as everyone knew was a crock but required by the insurance companies to avoid "sticky fingers."

The only saving grace was the command center did not need to have an oak tree trunk of transmission lines to maintain communication. Cell phones were all that were necessary. Everyone in the command center had a cell phone. The only hard wire communication was for the FAX machines, all three of them. Setting up the command center had been as fast as getting Formica tables and chairs in place.

That was the easy part.

The hard part was deciding who was in charge.

"Whoever is running this caper certainly knows human behavior," Archie said to Noonan looking across the command center.

"Oh, they know what they are doing, all right" Noonan replied. "From their end of the game, chaos is good. Chaos wastes time. It will take days for an operation like this to become efficient."

"We don't have days. We only have hours."

"Yup," replied Noonan as he peeled off his black leather jacket. "We've got less than a day."

"They said two days."

"That's what they said. My experience is that there are going to be a lot of hurdles we don't know about yet. We, as in you and me, only have about 24 hours to get things done. After 24 hours, they," Noonan said indicating the hubbub with his right hand, "will get organized. Right now, no one is in charge. The bomb in the Eads Bridge is smack dab over the center of the Mississippi River. It is not in either state's jurisdiction."

"Or either city's."

"Correct. There is going to be a scramble to see who is in charge. Worse, law enforcement wants to solve the crime, the insurance companies want to get paid and Homeland Security is in it for glory. That's the good news. The bad news is the families of the hostages have yet to figure out their loved ones are in harm's way. When they find out, well, that's when the fun is really going to begin."

"How's that?"

"Because then the media is going to get involved. Then it is going to get very messy very quickly."

"So we have to work faster.

"At warp speed."

Archie shook his head. "OK. But there is one thing bothering me. Why the bomb? The bad boys and girls have the hostages. Why do they need the bomb? This is basically a kidnapping. When there is a kidnapping the perps don't want any publicity. No cops, no interference. The perps just want it to be a simple transaction, money for people. So why the bomb?"

"I don't know," replied Noonan. "At least not yet. It's an odd piece of the puzzle. At this point, all I can surmise – and it's just a guess – the perps are going to release the hostages as soon as possible. Hostages are difficult to deal with. In kidnapping, when the victims are released the perps are no longer in control of the situation. With the bomb, they still have a card in the game after the hostages are released."

Archie was scratching his head. "That's a good guess but makes no sense. The perps are going to demand all the money before any hostages are released. Then there is going to be some kind of a 'wait until I get out town' before the hostages get released. Once the diamonds are transferred, the hostages have no value nor does the bomb."

"And this George character has to make a clean getaway." Noonan was clearly rolling possibilities over in his head. "I mean. We're going to be giving him diamonds. As in we are going to be putting diamonds in his hand. We may *not know* where the hostages are but we *will know* where George is. We'll have to keep him from giving us the slip."

"Absolutely," said Archie. "But I am sure our friends have a trick or two up their sleeve. We are a l-o-n-g way to before we are out of the weeds here. There are going to be a lot of moving parts to keep track of." Again, he gestured toward the rest of the warehouse.

Noonan agreed. "Granted a lot of things do not make any sense right now. All I can say is there are a lot of twists and turns ahead of us. The one thing we have to do is work faster than Homeland Security." Noonan also gestured back toward the crowded rooms. "The only thing I know for sure is the perps are going to make it as complicated as possible for us to do our job. Time is on their side. Anything and everything they can do to stall us even for a second is one second to their advantage. Eventually we will figure out who was involved. But they are gambling we won't figure it out fast enough to stop them. Three days from now they plan to be overseas with $50 million in diamonds."

CHAPTER 16

F BI agent Hastings – no first name because first names were the initial step on the road to a personal relationship – was roasting on the beach in Molokai when he got the call. Actually, his granddaughter got the call. That was because she had the official cell phone. When you are retired you don't want a cell phone. A cell phone is for the here-and-now and if there was any one thing retired FBI agent Hastings did not want it was any more here-and-now. After 37 years of here-and-now all he wanted was a beach as far as he could get from Washington D. C. and still speak English.

But when the corporate minions in Washington D. C. needed you, it wasn't far away enough.

"I'm not here," said into the cell phone he reluctantly took from his granddaughter's hand.

"It's George," said the voice on the other line, a voice he did not recognize.

" ."

It would have been "!" had he not spent 37 years with the Bureau. Work in the Bureau burns out the "!" and leaves you with "."

"He's back," the voice continued. "There's a Lear waiting for you at the Molokai Airport. We'll have credentials on location when you arrive. You will be landing at the East St. Louis Airport & Business Park."

"East St. Louis? *Missouri?*"

"Illinois. On the other side of the Mississippi."

"Does East St. Louis even have an airport?"

"Private field. They know you are coming. You will be briefed on the way."

"I'm supposed to be retired."

"You never retire from the FBI." Then the line went dead – even though a cell phone does not have a *line.*

CHAPTER 17

O ne afternoon a doctor was visited by a 75-year-old woman who wanted a prescription for birth control pills. The doctor kind of chuckled and asked why it was a 75-year-old woman would want birth control pills.

"They help me sleep better," the woman replied.

"That's interesting," replied the doctor. "I have never read birth control pills help anyone sleep better. Are you sure it's the birth control pills?"

"Absolutely," replied the elderly woman. "Every morning at breakfast I put one in my granddaughter's orange juice and I sleep better that night."

Reality is a matter of perception.

"Here's the latest out of East St. Louis," the Undersecretary of Homeland Security said as she handed a manila folder to each man. "Now we have 70 missing passengers and crew along with a bomb in the Eads Bridge. At this point Homeland Security is on point."

"We need to leave it that way," clipped Justice. "This has got to have the feel of terror." He paused, "for at least a week."

Defense agreed. "Our numbers are good in the swing states and terrorism is ringing bells from Peoria to Key West. We need to drag this out as long as possible."

"Is it possible?" Justice look at Homeland Security.

"It will be," replied Homeland Security. "It would be a whole lot easier – and more credible – if the press were to *discover* Justice had issued orders for snipers on the bridge." She had a sly smile when she said the word *discovered*.

"Done." Justice turned to Defense. "You are continuing those overflights for the dome cars, right?"

It was a nod rather than a verbal response.

"The press knows about the overflights?"

Again a nod rather than a verbal assenting.

"See if you can get your people in St. Louis to hint there is more here than just a robbery. I mean, this is one unusual robbery." Justice looked over his shoulder at White House. "What do we know about this George fellow? Anything my people can use?"

"Plans well and executes well. Three, four capers like this. Never been caught. In his 70s." Justice says.

"Well, let's make sure he doesn't get caught this time either. Terrorists don't get caught. They just fade away."

"Right now the FBI has one agent on the scene. He takes orders from Homeland Security. It should not be a problem."

CHAPTER 18

After three hours watching an empty rail line, Rabinowitz had been ordered back to headquarters. Where she sat for another hour waiting for an assignment.

"Rabinowitz," (Finally!) But the news was not so good. Yes, it was a commander, but not *the* Commander.

There was not a word of reference to her rank, just the order. "Rabinowitz, there's a special agent from the FBI arriving from Molokai within the hour. You will be working with him as long as this crisis lasts. I want the two of you hip-to-hip the whole time, do I make myself clear?"

Another cheeky assignment.

First she gets to sit in a patrol car watching an empty stretch of track for three hours. Then she sits in headquarters for an hour. Now she has to pick up a retired FBI agent from Molokai at the East St. Louis Airport & Business Park, a landing strip she did even know existed.

She grew up in East St. Louis – and East St. Louis was not exactly a bustling city.

This job had the stench of politics all over it. It also meant she was being sidelined again.

Rabinowitz nodded absentmindedly.

She didn't have to say anything in the affirmative because she was cheek-to-jowl with the commander. If there was any one adage which fit Rabinowitz like a glove it was life will occasionally throw you a curve. It was certainly the case here. Eight hours earlier she had been on routine patrol in East St. Louis when she was told to investigate a Winnebago on a railroad track crossing. Since then she'd been hijacked, kidnapped, forced to read bomb serial numbers and symbols making a VIN code seem like child's play. After she was released and made it back to her patrol vehicle, everyone in central command — from bottom to top —thought she had been smoking some powerful weed when she reported the bomb on its way to the Eads Bridge. It took top brass an hour to respond. Then it did what law enforcement always does: secured the scene too late to do anything productive and called for back-up which was too late and not needed. But the time call went out, there was nothing to secure and no reason for back-up. The boxcar with the bomb had been chained in place inside the bridge, the locomotive abandoned in the East St. Louis railyard. The perpetrators in the wind.

The combined forces of the law and order had done the right thing just very late. But Rabinowitz also realized it was also exactly what the perpetrators had expected.

And wanted.

The perps also expected the forces of law and order to keep the entire matter low-key. Low key, in this case, meant secret. The last thing anyone wanted was a full-scale panic. That was made clear to the authorities when a 70-something-year old man appeared in the office of the East St. Louis Mayor with the serial numbers for the bomb. He said his name was George, he wanted $50 million in diamonds and he was expected.

He also said the FBI knew all about him.

No one in City Hall believed George. Why should they? They didn't even know a bomb was in a bridge barely ten miles from their office.

They thought he was a nut.

They told him to peddle his soda crackers somewhere else and showed him the door.

He said he'd be outside on the park bench – waiting.

Everyone had laughed.

No one in City Hall had heard about the bomb or the missing train. Yet.

But there was at least one city employee with an IQ above room temperature. He called the FBI – just in case, you know, just in case.

After that, all hell broke loose.

"The FBI apparently knows this George character," the commander told Rabinowitz. "They've dealt with him before. In Alaska of all places. They tell us we should play ball with him. All he wants are diamonds. In Alaska, no one got hurt. We have to hope the same thing happens here."

"$50 million in gems is a lot, sir." When you are in the service, military or civilian, you must go with the flow. If you are standing with a superior officer, you say, "Sir." Or, "Ma'am." There were not a lot of Ma'ams yet. So, for the moment it was just "Sir."

"A lot of money to you and me, Rabinowitz. Not to the states of Illinois and Missouri." He pronounced 'Missouri' as 'Missour-uh.' "Not even a drop in the bucket of either state's budgets and a fraction of the cost of a new bridge. The question isn't if the states will pay but how fast."

"If the bomb is real."

"That's right, Officer." Anytime a superior used your title in a sentence, it was to end the conversation. "We have to assume the threat is real. The serial numbers you recorded match a device which was logged into a secure military facility in Los Alamos in the 1950s. It's gone. The military does not know where it is. It does not keep track of old weapons the way it does new ones. All they know for sure is the device with the specific serial number you copied is missing. Possibly misplaced. The serial codes match. We have no choice but to assume the device in the boxcar in the bridge is authentic."

"Yes, Sir." There are times when all you can say is "Yes, Sir."

"So what is our role, Sir? Is the FBI going to seize control of the operation?"

"If there is one iota of publicity, abso-positive-lutly. But not until we have done all the work. Your job is to keep this guy in check. Keep him in the loop and out of it. Get me?"

"It will take me a moment to figure that out," (pause) Sir."

"Work on it."

"I'm in the dark right now, sir." (There was "sir" again.) "What exactly is going on?"

"We'll need a crystal ball to figure it out. Right now, we are doing all we can. We are still looking for the dome cars. There's no reason to block the back tracks off the bridge because the terrorists . . ."

"Terrorists? I thought this was a simple extortion plot with a bomb."

"It's a lot more complicated than that now, Officer. We've got a twofer. Sometime over the past 12 hours 60 travel writers in railroad dome cars disappeared."

"The writers have disappeared or the dome cars?"

"Both."

Rabinowitz shook her head as if she were a cartoon character clearing her thoughts. "60 writer in three dome cars vanished? How can railway cars vanish?"

"They did not *vanish,* as in *poof,* Rabinowitz. But, as we speak, they are gone. The GPS on the entire train went ghost. There was no communication with the crew. It was just assumed there had been some kind of kerfuffle in the electronics."

"So the train never made it to where?"

"Chicago. It left here on time and never arrived in Chicago."

"And no one knows where it is?"

"Correct again."

"What about cell phones with the passengers. Surely someone on board . . ."

"Zip, Rabinowitz. No one knew the dome cars were missing until the railroad called the St. Louis Railroad police, or whatever they are called over there. They called us. To report 70 people missing, 60 travel writers and a train crew of 10."

"Could it have been some kind of accident?"

"None reported, Rabinowitz. Besides, this George fellow is saying he will release the hostages when he gets the first $10 million. Clearly the two events are linked. We have no choice but to keep collecting diamonds. As we collect the diamonds George is going to check them. We need at least $10 million within 36 hours and the balance at the end of 48."

"No ransom demands from anyone else?"

"Nope. Just this George fellow."

"I'm a bit confused, sir. You want me to pick up an FBI agent coming in from Molokai in the Hawaiian Islands and escort him around East St. Lewis to do what? And," she cut the commander off before he could answer her question, "what does any of this have to do with the missing dome cars or the bomb in the Eads Bridge or the collection of diamonds?"

"The answer to your first question, *Officer,*" the word *officer* accented in such a way to remind her she was speaking to a superior, "the extortionist named George is known to the FBI. George pulled off a similar extortion scheme in Anchorage, Alaska, a few years ago. This Agent Hastings was lead on the Alaska case. He will be helping us – *helping us*, officer, *helping us* – deal with George. The FBI agent is to be kept in the loop. Just kept in the loop. We do the heavy lifting. He's only here to advise."

"So we are dealing with this George? Do we know where this George is?"

"Yes. He's in the East St. Louis City Hall."

"City Hall?"

"City Hall."

"He is in City Hall waiting for the diamonds?"

"He is in City Hall waiting for the diamonds."

"It could be a long wait, sir."

"It can't be longer than about 40 hours and counting. George is waiting for his diamonds. You are waiting for this FBI agent to land. Everyone here," he said with a sweep of his hand, "is waiting for diamonds to show up."

"What about the dome cars and the travel writers?"

"That, Officer, is a very interesting question.

"I want to make sure I have this straight, (pause), sir," she said. "I am to pick up this FBI agent and deliver him to City Hall to talk to George."

"Affirmative."

"Sir, let me make sure I understand exactly what is happening. This George just walked into City Hall in East St. Louis with the same serial numbers I gave over the cell phone. He says he wants $50 million in gems. Diamonds. As we get the stones, he'll check them. He wants at least $10 million within 36 hours. Then he'll release the hostages. The second delivery is for the rest of the gems and he wants all gems within 48 hours. Then he'll disarm the bomb."

"That's what we know AWS."

"Do we trust him?"

There was a long moment of silence.

Finally, the commander spoke. "It's a happy day for jewelers, Officer. They are going to sell diamonds they got wholesale to two state governments retail and won't spend a penny of operating expense. Neither state is doing a lot of complaining because the insurance companies are going to pick up the tab. These perps know what they are doing. No one gets hurt, the insurance companies pick up the tab and recover their losses over a hundred thousand customers. Everyone ends up happy."

"If all ends well."

"Correct, Officer. If all ends well. Which is why you are going to be linked at the hip with Agent Hastings. Where he goes, you go. I want you standing by the urinal when he takes a piss. That's how close I want you to be."

"Yes, sir."

"That does not sound like an enthusiastic 'Yes, sir.'"

"Yes, sir. If the agent goes to a urinal, I'll be right there with him."

"The reference to the urinal was a figure of speech, Officer. But you get my point."

"Yes, sir."

"Good. You are our most important asset right now. You've been on-site. You've talked with the perps. Keep your eyes and ears open. This may be a short extortion, er, terrorist act, but we are likely to be chasing these *terrorists* for years."

"Yes, sir."

"Agent Hastings will be landing within the hour."

"It will take him some time to get here, traffic and all."

"He's landing at the East St. Louis airport."

Rabinowitz paused for a moment. "There is no East St. Louis airport."

"Well, there sort of is. It's the East St. Louis Airport & Business Park. Rich folks use it. It's not for the commercial traveler."

"OK. How will I recognize him?"

"He'll be the only person getting off a Lear jet. The FBI pulled him out of retirement and off the beach in Molokai. I'll bet he's fit, tanned, wearing sandals, khaki trousers and a Tony Bahama print shirt. He might even be wearing a lei. Maybe he'll have a boa constrictor around his neck and a Mai Tai in each hand. *I don't know, Rabinowitz.* He's coming in. You're to meet him. You are to stay with him. Hip-to-hip. It's your job. Get to it."

CHAPTER 19

Alaskan humorist Warren Sitka is famous for many statements. Perhaps the most quoted – and most often told by members of the Alaska Legislature to their compeers across the aisle – is to "Never pass up an opportunity to sit down and shut up when you don't know what you are talking about."

One of the greatest drawbacks to being young was you did not have the life experience to realize real life is unorganized. When you are young, this does not appear to be the case. When you get a job you quickly discover that everything at the state or company is organized. There is a chain of command. It was established before you arrived and "that is the way we do things around here." Someone must lead (the boss or supervisor) and the others (everybody else) must follow. This, however, is a very jaundiced – but true – view of life because wherever you go there is already a chain of command. It's the way things work. It's called *organization.*

Except for three kinds of people: stockbrokers, fine artists and travel writers.

Stockbrokers are people who do not believe in Santa Claus or Leprechauns but still think they can beat Wall Street. Fine artists talk about the "inner spirit coming through on canvas" but keep painting the kind of schlock that will sell. Travel writers are God's gift – or the gods' gift – to the world of the unwashed because they are paid to tell their readers about places the readers will never go. Travel writers are special because they get free liquor on complimentary trips and no one has a nasty thing to say to them. They are at the top of their game and none of them are over 45. If they are over 45, they are called editors.

There were no stockbrokers or fine artists on the Bonanza Travel Agency list of guests. Just travel writers. All under 45. Herding cats was more productive than getting the travel writers organized into a cohesive unit – which Whittaker never could – and the best the group of 70 could do was get the travel writers to light three fires in a row so no one watching would mistake one fire for a solitary camper. There was not a single former Boy or Girl Scout onboard or a military veteran within the group therefore, sadly, "three fires in a straight line" meant nothing to the hostages. No one was in charge because *everyone* was in charge there ended up five fires which, predictably, became one when the non-veteran Boy or Girl Scouts did not bother to clear the area around the original fires down to bare earth. Consequently, the fires popped to life and ate their way – all five of them – jackrabbit fast and took down the three structures which the hostages could have used for shelter.

Along with the buildings went the food supplies and toilets.

When the fires went out, the water pipes and faucet were still available.

But the buildings were gone.

And every travel writer was blaming every other travel writer for the disaster.

And then it began to rain.

CHAPTER 20

Agent Hastings — and that was what he demanded to be called, *Agent* as if it was his first name or a substitute for *Mr.* — had the personality of a log. But only when he was on duty. He was actually a very jovial fellow. In private. In retirement. But on the job he was all business with not an ounce of humor and not one to crack a joke. When it came to humor he was like an engineer. As the saying goes, the difference between an engineer and a computer is the computer has a personality.

But he was very good at his job.

Very good.

Even better, he was proficient while those around him were losing their edge because of the pressure. He was exactly the person you wanted defusing a bomb because he did not feel the rising tension of the downward ticking fuse clock.

Even more important, he was an expert on George. He and George had crossed paths before. Twice. Once it was in the aftermath. But once he and George had negotiated. Face-to-face.

Agent Hastings did not need to go over any case file notes of his encounter with George. Every second of that confrontation, all 70-odd hours of it, had been indelibly seared into his psyche. But it was not the act that caused the scorching; George had gotten away with it. In Agent Hasting's entire career, only one man had *gotten away with it*: George. Further, George had gotten away with it *big time*. George and as many as ten men had held an entire city of 500,000 hostage. For three days. Then they skedaddled with give-or-take $15 million in gems. Agent

Hastings only caught one of the gang, a corrupt jeweler who got a good lawyer and slipped through the judicial system.

So, it was crooks a BIG ONE and the forces of law and order ZIP.

Agent Hastings did not like zip. The forces of law and order get a lot of zips. You can arrest 'em but you cannot convict them. Some of them just get away. But George had gotten away on Hastings' watch. HIS! Not some other agent in some other city. HIS! This did not sit well with Agent Hastings. Even in retirement. It never would sit well.

Not only that, George had also gotten away with millions. The one blemish on Agent Hastings's record. It didn't matter to Agent Hastings that other agents had lost a few along the way. That was them. He was Agent Hastings. He wanted to live out his retirement with a clean record. It just wasn't going to happen. George had ruined a pleasant retirement.

Then, one day, while he was lying on the beach in Molokai, God gave him a second chance. Now he was on his way back into the game.

George was back.

When he arrived in East St. Louis, Agent Hastings was out the door and onto the tarmac even as the plane was still rolling to a stop. That was how bad he wanted back in the game.

Now he was here in East St. Louis.

George was here.

Let the game begin.

There had been an Illinois State Trooper – Patrolwoman, rather – waiting for him on the landing strip. Where he had landed could hardly have been called an airport. In fact, it was not. It was a landing strip for rich people with planes who wanted to commute by air to St. Louis – both of them.

The patrol cruiser had been moving toward him as he walked. He thought this was most excellent. He didn't have time to waste and whomever was in that vehicle knew how short time was. He hoped it was this officer Rabinowitz. She was the one who had taken down all the information on the bomb. At least it wasn't a nuclear device. He had cleared that with the Atomic Energy Commission. It was more of a back-up to a back-up. A conventional bomb. Big but still conventional. Even so, it would still take out the bridge right down to its foundation.

Agent Hastings didn't see it happening that way. George was a very smart cookie. He wanted the diamonds and the adventure and then he wanted to get gone. Be gone. Long gone.

The last time Agent Hastings had seen him, George had said he was in his mid-70s. That was seven years earlier; George would be pushing 80 now. At least. It was about the age of the man who showed up in the office of the Mayor of East St. Louis.

"That scoundrel," Agent Hastings kept mumbling under his breath every few seconds. "That scoundrel," He half-hated the man for what he had done and half-loved the crook for this one last chance to catch him in the act and send him to prison for the rest of his life. "That scoundrel! That scoundrel!" Which was as close to a profanity as he allowed himself.

Agent Hastings gave no indication he cared whether his contact with the Illinois State Troopers was a woman or a man. If he cared, he didn't say so. But then again, he didn't ever say much at all. Woman, man, all that mattered was the uniform. Rabinowitz extended her hand which Agent Hasting shook casually. It was as friendly as he ever got in the field. But he shook it as he was getting into the patrol cruiser. After the vehicle started he said, "We are going to the Mayor's Office, yes?"

"I've been told to take you where you want to go."

Agent Hastings did not reply. He just kind of grunted. Then he said, "AWS where are we?"

"As We Speak," said Rabinowitz who had only been recently briefed regarding FBI acronyms and protocol, "there are 70 travel writer and railroad crew in three dome railway cars missing somewhere between St. Louis and Chicago. An aerial search is underway but nothing has turned up. There is a bomb on the railroad tracks of the Eads Bridge over the Mississippi River and the railway has been blocked on both sides of the river. At this moment, only law enforcement, governors' offices and the Mayor Office in East St. Louis know what is happening."

"That will change soon enough," snapped Agent Hastings.

"How do you know that, sir?"

"I know the man involved. He is a master at confusion. When he needs chaos; the media will be informed. Then all kinds of confusion will occur. That's his escape plan."

Rabinowitz was silent for a moment. "Is that what he did in Alaska?"

Agent Hastings did not answer directly. He side-slipped, "George is a master of organized chaos."

"George?"

"Officer! This is an FBI operation, start to finish. I can appreciate your concern but events are moving very fast. I don't have time to give you a complete rundown of the FBI's contact with George. Let's just say it is extensive. This will be his fourth terrorist act." Agent Hastings was careful to accent the word *terrorist*. "We didn't catch up with him until the third act. That was in Anchorage and because it is similar to what is transpiring here, I will give you a thumbnail."

"A thumbnail would be a good start, (pause) sir."

"No reason to think I'm holding out on you, officer. The *sir* is not required. Just refer to me as Agent Hastings, no first name. Just Agent Hastings. I'm not your boss and I'm not your friend. I'm your partner as long as this lasts. Let's make sure we have this straight. With George, when things happen they move fast and I cannot" – he paused for emphasis – "we cannot let our personalities slow us down."

"Ok, Agent Hastings. What can you tell me about George?"

"In a nutshell, he is *very* good at what he does. His ploy here is very similar to what he did in Anchorage. In Anchorage he held the entire city hostage."

"A whole city? How'd he do that?"

"He took control of an abandoned nuclear missile silo overlooking the city. He moved in some ground-to-ground missiles and held the local airport and two military landing strips hostage. Then he threatened to blow up the electric utility. It was the middle of winter with temperatures about ten below zero. Not a friendly fellow."

"So he'd freeze the city?"

"In essence."

"So he was holding the city hostage. Did he ask for gems?"

"$50 million. The city paid."

"Just like here."

"That's right. No one cared. The gems were insured which means no one was out a dime."

"Except the insurance companies."

"Insurance companies never lose."

"Sounds awfully familiar. Those guys in the nuclear missile silo. How did they get away?"

"We're not sure. They either took off in some Harriers, the . . ."

"Those vertical take-off and landing planes?"

"Right. They either left by Harrier or simply got lost in the crowd of military personnel who descended on the nuclear missile silo. There were no security cameras on the silo and everyone was hitching rides with whatever vehicle was there. It would have been easy for his men – about four of them by our count – to simply get lost in the shuffle. We did find an abandoned vehicle but with so many trucks and sedans involved, one or two out of place was no big deal. No, we don't know what happened to them. They vanished into thin air."

"What about George?"

"He was in a downtown hotel checking the diamonds to make sure they were genuine. When he wanted to go, he just left in the one direction we didn't have covered: up."

"Up? You mean he left by helicopter?"

"No, he was snatched off the roof of the hotel. Maybe. Days later we found a rope down the side of the hotel. He may have rappelled down to a first-floor platform, the top of the kitchen, picked the lock on the outside roof door and walked out through the hotel. No one knew what he looked like. As a result, no one knew who to look for. Again, poof, and he was gone."

"You never saw him again."

"Correct. Just poof and gone." Agent Hastings made a gesture of a *poof* by throwing up his hands and extending them to the side. "*Poof* and gone."

"This is not good news. That is, when someone, an individual, can pull off a heist that large and disappear it is not good news."

"That's right. But the advantage we have now is we know what he is going to do. He is going to get the diamonds. The real trick is going to stop him and his men before they all disappear."

"Anything else you can tell me to keep me prepared?'

"Do not underestimate George. He is a very clever man. He has the entire caper planned to the second. He knows what he is doing. The best we can do is slow things down as much as possible. Somewhere in his plan is an unmovable item, a time-related piece of the puzzle which cannot be altered. Whatever it is, he must hit that schedule dead-on. For a starter, I'd suggest the command center put together a list of everything which has a specific, set time. Not something just planned but something which has been set for a long period of time."

"You mean like a theater opening or a basketball game?"

"Something like that. It has to involve enough people who do not know each other that George and his cronies can fade into the crowd."

"No getaway in a fast car?"

"That's not the way George works. He just disappears. How he gets out of town is anyone's guess. Anchorage only has one airport and one road out of town. He just disappeared. He might have had a safe house and just holed up for a week. We don't know. We're pretty sure he didn't fly out the night he got the diamonds because we looked – I looked – at all of the security tapes from the airport and I did not see George. I didn't get a good look at him but I saw him clearly enough to recognize him on tape. I got zip. Don't take anything for granted when it comes to George. He is amazingly resourceful. Be prepared for anything."

"OK. But what's on the agenda first?"

"We talk to George."

CHAPTER 21

Neither Noonan nor Archie was surprised when the three dome cars turned up.

"What a surprise," said Archie when he was told the three dome cars had been discovered. He waved the note with the heading, in large letters – Italicized – JOINT HOMELAND SECURITY COMMIS-SION – and beneath the title was a listing of three states. "Of course, we were the last ones to be informed."

Noonan made a mock face of surprise and shook his head. "Of course. We are doing exactly what the bad boys and girls want us to do. I'm not surprised the dome cars have been found. I'm guessing there wasn't a clue as to where they have been."

Archie was silent for a moment as he read the note. "It's another one of those 'yes and no' answers. When the dome cars did not arrive in Chicago on time, relatives began calling the police."

"No surprise there," Noonan said. "I'll bet they called the cell phones of the writers as well," Noonan added.

"Yup. The police traced the cell phones to their location."

"Uh, huh," replied Noonan. "This would be too easy. Let me guess. That's the 'yes' part of the answer. The 'no' part is the phones are in a various location and scattered geographically."

"That's a 'yes.' The phones were located all over the map. My guess is the writers and crew had their cell phones taken from them and then the cell phones were sent all over the two states by FedEx and UPS. With the right mailing labels they would just go. If a phone in a FedEx box was sent to a large company it would take days for some company to figure out the package was bogus."

Noonan nodded sadly. "I'm also betting when we investigate who sent the packages it will be a bogus company."

"Correct. It already has been investigated. The company is Midnight, Inc., It is a company that does not exist. It is headquartered in a mailbox in a FedEx office in East St. Louis. The ID used to establish the box was a California Driver's License which is bogus. The FedEx account was established in East St. Louis and payment was made by an East St. Louis bank,. . "

Noonan finished his sentence, "established with the same California driver's license."

"Yup."

"And the bank account was started with a few hundred dollars in cash and regular cash deposits were made."

"Yup, again."

"And all withdrawals were made by debit card — ergo no signatures."

"You've been here before!"

"No. These guys are professionals. They know exactly what they are doing. This caper has been planned right down to the paper clips."

Archie kept waving the note. "There's more. The dome cars have been found."

"It would be pretty hard to hide dome cars."

"So they didn't. They uncoupled the cars and attached them to box cars waiting to be switched to passing trains. One showed up in Chicago. The railroad people are trying to trace it back to where it might have been picked up. The other two have yet to be found."

"So the dome cars probably went in three different directions. That would not be hard if you knew what you were doing." Noonan scratched his head. "These perps know the railroad system well enough scrambling the paperwork would not have been hard."

"My guess too," replied Archie. "They don't care if we find out who they are as long as we do not find out for a day or two. By then they will be gone."

"Like I said," Noonan said. "These are smart cookies. They have the cell phones which are traceable scattered and then they distributed the dome cars on other trains. Even if we can trace the dome cars back to where they were switched it is going to take time."

"You are right. It will take time."

"True. The key here is to find the hostages. It doesn't matter where the dome cars are located. We'll find all of them soon enough. We need to find the hostages."

"Where do you think they are?"

"I hate to ask," Noonan said pointing at the note, "has the aerial search been called off?"

Archie looked at the note. "It doesn't say."

"We'd better make sure they keep looking."

"What for? We've found the dome cars."

"The locomotive. If you know what you are doing – and these people seem to know exactly what they are doing – dividing up three cars and attaching them onto other strings of box cars would not be hard. But you can't do that with a locomotive. The locomotive is going to have to stay where it is. Once we find the locomotive we'll know where to start looking for the hostages."

Archie shook his head. "I don't know much about trains but it would be very difficult to find one locomotive on those thousands of miles of track."

"Piece of cake," Noonan replied. "There will not be many loco-motives out there. If the pilot spots one not moving, he radios in the location. If the locomotive has an active GPS, it can be eliminated."

"Suppose the locomotive is in a tunnel or under a bridge?"

"Unlikely. I'll bet Illinois is all flatland between here and Chicago. There can't be a lot of tunnels. Even if there were, those tunnels would be on active tracks. Railways under bridges are the same. This locomotive is sitting in some railyard on spur tracks. Once we find it we'll have a starting point for the hostages."

"It gives us a place to start for sure."

"We don't have a lot of time. The clock is ticking. I've been here before."

Archie scratched his head. "So far everything has been quiet. The relatives of the hostages have been told to stay calm and wait. They've been put up at the Bond Hotel here in East St. Louis. An old and venerable establishment."

"Let me guess, the railway company is footing the bill."

"Absolutely. It doesn't want any law suits."

Noonan gave Archie a hard took. "Take it from me, the voice of experience. Those relatives are not going to stay calm and wait for very long. Once the press gets wind of what is going on there are going to camera crews on every mile of railway between here and Timbuktu."

Archie smiled. "Timbuktu is quite a ways from here but I know what you mean. Once the press gets involved …"

"Which is why we have to move fast. When we find the locomotive we should be able to find the hostages rather quickly. I mean, it's going to take a large building to hold 70 people. I'm betting the hostages have been left alone."

"Which means they are only a bargaining chip in the generic."

"I'm guessing that's the case. This George fellow, that's his name, right?"

"So I've been told."

"This George is demanding $50 million in gems. As we get the stones, we have him appraise them. When he gets the first $15 million he will release the hostages. He'll live up to his promise because none of his people are where the hostages are. He's gambling we're going to focus our manpower on the hostages, not the bomb."

"He's right," Archie replied. "That's the way law enforcement works. People first."

Noonan would have loved to swivel around in his chair but the metal monstrosity in which he was sitting did not give him the option. "Archie, with George we need to play his game. We need to get into his head."

"I'm game. What do you think is in his head?"

"Not what. Who. David Copperfield."

CHAPTER 22

W hat do you mean we must keep looking for the locomotive," snapped Lizzard when Noonan gave him the bad news. "What good is the locomotive if we've found the dome cars?"

"Because the locomotive is the key to the hostages."

"How's that?"

"Because the perpetrators were . . ."

"Terrorist."

"OK, terrorists, were able to unhook the dome cars and hide them in strings of boxcars. It would be easy if you had a locomotive and time. But you cannot hide the locomotive that easily. It's not on a mainline. If it were, it would have been spotted. It's hidden in plain sight."

Lizzard's eyes lit up. "'Hidden in plain sight.' I like that. I'll use that."

Noonan smiled slyly. "Absolutely, Commissioner Lizzard. See, sir," – and it galled Noonan through the bone to the marrow to say *sir* – "the key to finding the hostages is the locomotive. The dome cars were scattered because they could be. But the locomotive is sitting in place because the perpe . . ."

"Terrorists."

"Terrorists, yes, sir, because it cannot be moved without attracting attention. It is clearly hidden in plain sight. The perp, er, terrorists, expect us to be concentrating on trying to find the dome cars and tracing them back to where they were latched onto the different strings of boxcars. They know it will take time. They are trying to get us to focus on the wrong clue. They want us to stop looking for the locomotive."

"What will finding the locomotive give us?"

"The hostages."

This instantly caught Lizzard's attention. Noonan knew because the pitch of Lizzard's voice went from haggard to interested. Lizzard's eyes flashed PR.

"Hostages?"

"See, sir, wherever the hostages are, they were taken out of the dome cars where the locomotive is. The dome cars were scattered because they could be. But the locomotive is hidden in plain sight. The hostages had to have been moved by bus – or buses – to another location. But the other location must be near where the locomotive is right now. The terrorists could not afford to bus the hostages one hundred miles to a secure location. Wherever they are, the hostages are very close to where the locomotive is right now."

Lizzard thought for a moment. "That makes sense."

"Yes, sir. The smart thing to do is to find the locomotive."

"How can we do that? The aerial flights have been stopped."

Noonan took a moment and then let a false thought raise his eyebrows. "Well, if you can't look for the locomotive from the air, why not do it from the ground?"

"From the ground? How would I do that?"

"Well, why not have the Joint Homeland Security Commission hold a press conference and ask for the help of the public. Ask the public to report every locomotive standing alone in a rail yard to your office. Once you find the location of the locomotive you can send ground troops into the area to look for the hostages."

"Suppose I, we, do find the locomotive. How does it lead us to the hostages? They could be anywhere."

"Actually, sir, that's not accurate. See, if there are 70 hostages they are being held in a large, secure structure. When you find the locomotive, you start looking for large structures, within 20 miles of the rail line. It might be an abandoned steel mill, deserted military base, sanitarium whatever. It should be large and will be guarded. When you find it you surround the structure. Then you've turned the tables on the terrorist. Now they're the hostages."

Lizzard's mind was clearly clicking. "That would take a lot of manpower."

"It would also give the Joint Homeland Security Commission a way to introduce itself to the public."

Lizzard smiled.

Noonan continued, "Someone is going to have to deal with the relatives of the hostages and the press. The Joint Homeland Security Commission would seem to be the logical choice. When it comes to terrorism, as you have always said, it's a national priority. Maybe you could even ask Washington for money for this emergency."

"A capital idea, Noonan. A capital idea." Lizzard was giddy with excitement.

CHAPTER 23

"You are one sly dog, you are, you are." Archie was chuckling when Noonan told him the Joint Homeland Security Commission was going to be looking for the hostages.

Noonan smiled. "Yes, it's a ruse but it is not going to last very long. Those hostages are going to turn up quickly. This entire matter is going to end rapidly – about 40 hours at the longest. Right now there are five stumbling blocks. Three of them are now out of our hair: the Joint Homeland Security Commission is on a wild goose chase taking the press and a lot of boots on the ground are with them. Sure, they will find the hostages. But it will take time. Every second of time they waste looking for the hostages is time we have without the Commission breathing down out necks to solve the last two problems: paying the ransom and stopping the perpetrators before they abscond with the diamonds."

"Clever. The press is going to be chasing the hostages. Which leaves us in the clear to do our job."

"Almost clear. We still have to deal with the FBI. It has flown in an agent from Hawaii. Apparently, this person has dealt with George, that's his name, right?"

"Yup, George."

"This agent has dealt with George before?"

"Yup."

"Why didn't he catch George the last time?"

"Good question. We'll ask him when we meet with him. Right now, we need to know how many diamonds have been collected. I'm betting this George fellow is not going to wait around for two shipments. He's going to say something along the lines of time being of the essence and he wants all the stones at the same time. Particularly when the hostages are found."

"Clever. I'll bet he planned to take what stones he has and beat feet while we run around like chickens with our heads cut off looking for the hostages. He probably figures he can give us the bomb codes and still use the hostages as a negotiating chip. He leaves and tells us later where the hostages are."

"If we don't move fast, he will do exactly that."

CHAPTER 24

Contrary to popular believe, there is an upside to incompetence. The prevailing view is an incompetent person gets what he/she deserves and that is as far as it goes. This leaves the listener to assume the incompetent person is stewing in his/her own juices and this is his/her just desserts. Even more important, if the incompetent were high-and-mighty, then this would be his/her comeuppance and he/she got what was coming.

Ah, if reality were so cut and dry.

But it is not.

Incompetence is a reward, not a punishment. Incompetent people usually have their chestnuts pulled from the fire and forever after they will say how they had planned the rescue of the matter. They did not *make* a mistake, God forbid, they had merely set in motion a clever plan, a plan only someone with their brainpower could have conceived.

Like a forest ranger investigating a brush fire.

At an abandoned Federal mental hospital.

And then finding 70 people shivering in the rain. None of them with overcoats, cell phones or computers. Not even a pencil or pen among all of them. Who needed pencils or pens when you had cell phones and computers?

Chapter 25

"You are going to have to play lead on this," Archie said to Noonan as they poured over a map of the Eads Bridge. "I've never done anything like this before."

"Neither have I," replied Noonan. "Looking over this blueprint tells me nothing at all."

"Then why are we doing it?"

Noonan looked over Archie's shoulder in the direction of the warehouse Command Center. "To keep our friends from Homeland Security happy. They wanted us to look over a blueprint of the bridge. And now we have looked over a blueprint of the bridge."

"That's all fine and good, but it doesn't get us one step closer to finding the hostages or defusing the bomb."

"True. Let's forget about the hostages. Homeland Security is stumbling after them. I doubt the hostages are in danger. They are simply a distraction. Let's concentrate on what's important."

"The bomb."

"No. The bomb is another distraction. The perps are just tossing things in our way, things to keep us busy. There are only three things which are important. First, is the collection of diamonds. Second, delivery of the diamonds to this George fellow. Third, George getting away with the diamonds. All we can do is start slowing down the first two. At the very least it will throw a monkey wrench into their plans. What we need to do is figure out how George is going to try to get away."

"I just figured he was going to take the diamonds and give us the code after he was long gone."

Noonan smiled. "It's a dangerous game he's playing. He knows we are not going to give him the diamonds unless he gives us the code and he knows we are going to check the code to make sure it's authentic. No matter what, the bomb has to be disarmed before he gets the diamonds."

"That's why he's got the hostages. It's his ace in the hole."

"I doubt it. He's got to know we are going to find those hostages quickly. The hostages are only a delaying tactic. It will keep lots of cops busy for 24 hours. Then he must come up with another delaying tactic for the next 24 hours. We've got less than 40 hours to solve this."

"How do you think he's going to make his getaway?"

"That, Archie, is our job to figure out."

CHAPTER 26

Rabinowitz and Agent Hastings – and Agent Hastings kept demanding she refer to him as *Agent Hasting* – had no difficulty finding George. He was exactly where they expected to find him: in an empty office on the third floor of the East St. Louis City Hall. He was seated on a metal folding chair behind a dilapidated wooden desk which had seen its best days before the Civil War. There was a black velvet cloth on the surface of the desk and George was using a loupe to examine diamonds one at a time from a pile which looked like a miniature pyramid.

George was dressed casually. He was wearing a striped shirt and jeans and there was a battered leather briefcase on the edge of the desk. Other than the diamonds and the briefcase, the only other object on the surface of the table was a .45. To Rabinowitz, George was the most unassuming perp she had ever seen. At his youngest he was in his upper 70s. His hair was completely white even though he had a salt-and-pepper mustache. His hands were gnarly as if he had been a workman during this his non-criminal life. Beneath the latex gloves on his left hand was a gold wedding band on ring finger of his left hand. Beneath the latex glove on his right hand was a signet ring on his right-hand ring finger. The top of a white undershirt peeked out at his neckline.

To Rabinowitz, George was avuncular. He looked just like everyone's favorite uncle. He was the kind of an uncle who could be mistaken for Teddy Roosevelt and was always quick with a laugh and story about the old days. His face was cheerful and he brightened when she and Agent Hastings came into the room.

"Agent Hasting!" George was enthusiastically friendly as Rabinowitz and Agent Hastings entered the room. "I've been expecting you."

"So we meet again," said Agent Hastings in the clear, FBI-professional, no-nonsense, flat tone agents practice for years to be cookiecutter identical with every other agent in the field.

"Come on!" said George. "Show a little enthusiasm! After all, we are old friends."

"We're not friends, George. You're a perp and I'm going to bring you in."

"Of course you are, Agent Hastings, of course you are." Then George looked at Rabinowitz and said confidentially. "The FBI." He threw his hands up in mock frustration. "The same everywhere. I'm George. I'd shake your hand but as you can see, I'm a bit busy here." His left hand swept over the table.

Rabinowitz noticed he kept his right hand near the .45.

George noticed she noticed.

"Ah, yes, officer. The gun. You see the gun. Well let me put your mind at ease. It's not for people like you. It's for the heroes who show up occasionally. As Agent Hastings will tell you, I do not shoot people. I just take their diamonds. And you are . . .?" He let the sentence hang.

"You mean my name?" asked Rabinowitz.

"Of course! I know Agent Hastings by name. We're old friends."

"Not so," snapped Agent Hastings. "We need to get down to business, George."

"Patience, Agent Hastings. We've got all of," he said as he paused to look at his wrist for his watch. The movement was for show because he had no watch on his wrist. "All of, goodness me, I forget to put on my watch." He looked at Rabinowitz. "So we have time to be pleasant. You are . . .? Again, he let the sentence hang.

"Rabinowitz."

"You have a first name?"

"Rabinowitz is fine."

"Another stick in the mud. OK, Rabinowitz it is. Now, Rabinowitz, here's how this matter is going to play out. I don't have to tell Agent Hastings because he has been through the wringer before. You are to bring the diamonds from wherever you are collecting them to me. I check them for authenticity and quality. When I get at least $10 million, you get the location of the hostages. When I get $50 million I give you the code to disarm the bomb."

"And you are just going to walk away with the diamonds?"

"Of course, dear lady! That's the way it works."

Rabinowitz shook her head. "You can't possibly think we are going to give you the diamonds and let you leave without making sure the bomb is disarmed."

"True, true," said George. "But that's all in the future, officer Rabinowitz. We are a long way from the *denouement*. There are already some complications."

"Complications?" cut in Agent Hastings.

"Of course, Agent Hastings. You remember the joy we had together in Anchorage when some false stones were slipped in with the real ones?"

Agent Hastings was silent for a long moment.

"I take your silence to mean *yes*. Well, you have some rather unscrupulous jewelers in either – and probably both – St. Louis and East St. Louis." He pointed to a small pile of gems on the left of the gleaming pyramid of gems. It seems – as in Anchorage – some of your reputable jewelers are slipping in garbage. I am sure they figured when I asked for diamonds of quality they could pull a fast one. So they did. Or tried. These stones," he said as he pointed to the pile, "are worthless for the ransom. Return them, replace them and don't let it happen again."

"You won't get away with this, you know." Again, it was the same FBI-measured tone from Agent Hastings.

"Yes, yes, yes," George said quickly. "We went over this before, Agent Hastings. Now, why don't you be a good little FBI agent and let me talk with Rabinowitz alone."

Agent Hasting clearly did not like this at all. He started to say something but Rabinowitz politely cut him off. "I'll be just fine. I'll see you in the hall."

Agent Hastings stalled for a moment and then, with a show of great reluctance, backed out into the hallway. He shut the door behind him.

"FBI agents," snorted George. "They are all the same."

"You're not going to get away with this," Rabinowitz replied professionally. "Why not give it up now before anyone gets hurt?"

"Rabinowitz! I'm surprised! You're sounding like an FBI agent. Please don't go down the same path! At least not while we are working together."

"We're not working together."

"Of course we are! You're much more personable than Agent Hastings. You are going to be the go-between me and the rest of the law enforcement gang."

"We're not a gang."

"Ok, the law enforcement rabble. I need a cool-head between me and them. You seem to be that person. You see," George said as he looked down and scooped up a small handful of stones and dropped them into a handkerchief and tied the ends. Then he handed the bundled handkerchief to Rabinowitz. "When bad stones are mixed with the good," he waggled the index finger of his right hand back and forth as if to say *bad boy* to a dog, "it puts everything at risk. Here," he handed Rabinowitz the handkerchief bundle. "Take these stones back to the command center or whatever you call it and tell them to be more careful. Every second of delay on my end is dangerous." Rabinowitz took the handkerchief bundle from George's hand as he scooped up some stones from the pyramid and put them in a black fabric bag. "As long as authentic stones like these," he shook the bag, "continue to go into my briefcase," he said indicating the attaché, "all is well."

"Just out of curiosity," Rabinowitz started.

George cut her off. "George."

"OK, George, just out of curiosity. How are you going to get away with the diamonds after you have given us the code to disarm the bomb?"

"That, my dear Rabinowitz, is going to be a surprise."

CHAPTER 27

Rabinowitz barely made it into the hallway before she was snagged by a guy old enough to be her grandfather and a man the age of her younger brother. It was a real Mutt-and-Jeff but on the upside. The old guy was the small one but he was still a good six feet tall. The other was a skyscraper. Before she could say anything, Agent Hastings pulled her into the Mayor's waiting room.

"This is Archibald Yenokovian, one of your Illinois State Troopers," Agent Hastings said indicating the younger of the two. "The other is Captain Heinz Noonan of the Sandersonville Police Department."

"Sandersonville?" She was clearly confused. "Where's that?"

"North Carolina," said Noonan quickly. "You might say I'm here on loan."

"That's quite a ways for a loan," Rabinowitz said.

"True, true," replied Noonan. "But at this point no one is very picky about who's helping."

"Well," replied Rabinowitz, "I am. We don't need any cowboys here right now."

Archie was about to say something but Noonan cut him off. "A fair statement. Many people consider me a specialist on crimes which are odd or unusual. Like this one. We have a train which has vanished, 70 people missing, a ticking time bomb and a guy named George who appeared out of thin air demanding $50 million in diamonds. Just your usual crime in East St. Louis."

"Well, it's odd all right," returned Rabinowitz. "But you are not in my chain of command."

"Nope," said Archie. "And we don't want to be. We just want to know everything that was said in there." He indicated George's room door.

"Don't leave anything out," Agent Hastings icily warned.

Rabinowitz gave Agent Hastings an Arctic stare. Then she handed him the bundled handkerchief. "What he said was these gems were inferior or fake. I'm not a jeweler. I don't know the difference. He said he wanted all the stones and then he would release the hostage and give us the code for the bomb."

"Nothing else?" Archie cut in. "That's it? He talks to you alone and that's all he says?"

Noonan put his hand on Archie's arm. "Now, Archie, let's take a bit of time here." Then, to Rabinowitz, he added, "It's not what George said that's important. It's what he did."

"How's that?" Archie clearly had a confused look on his face.

"This George is a very cleverly fellow, Archie. Very clever fellows do not want to deal with other very clever people. Remember Agent Hastings said George wanted to talk with Rabinowitz alone?" Noonan indicated Agent Hastings standing stolid against a wall. Archie nodded agreement. "Why do you think George did NOT want to talk to Agent Hastings but DID want to talk with officer Rabinowitz?"

Archie's face gave every indication he had absolutely no idea why.

"Because," Noonan continued. "Agent Hastings is a professional. He has had years of experience dealing with perps. He can read them like a book. Rabinowitz," Noonan gestured toward her, "does not have that kind of experience. She misses things an experienced investigator would pick up. Not to slight your ability," Noonan said to Rabinowitz as he turned toward her.

"I'm not offended, Captain, Captain. . ."

"Heinz. Just call me Heinz."

"OK, Heinz. George didn't tell me anything we don't already know. He had a big pile of diamonds he was going through one at a time and a little pile of stones to the side. He said the little pile of stones were flawed or fake. He said this was because the jewelers were asked for high quality diamonds and some of the jewelers slipped in the flawed or fake diamonds. He scooped those diamonds up, put them in a handkerchief and gave them to me. That's the bundle I gave Agent Hastings."

"Did George actually use the word flawed or fake?" asked Agent Hastings as he pointed at the handkerchief in her hand.

"No. I believe he said *false*. Then he said the stones were unacceptable for the ransom."

"I see," continued Hastings. "But the other stones were acceptable?"

"He never said that word. The word he used was *authentic*. He scooped up a small handful of stones and put them in a little black bag. I'm guessing it was velvet like the black cloth which covered the tabletop."

"You saw him put the diamonds in the black velvet bag?" Noonan asked.

"Yes, sir, er Heinz. He scooped up a small handful of diamonds from the edge of the pile, of a pyramid-shaped pile and put the stones in the little bag. He tied the bag shut and put it in a leather briefcase he had on the table."

"You're sure he didn't palm the diamonds?" Noonan asked.

"Why?" Agent Hasting cut in. "Why would George play a magic trick? He had stones and must get them out of the building. He can't very well walk out of the building with $50 million in diamonds in his pants pocket."

"I don't know," replied Noonan. "All I do know is George has been planning this for a long time. Every detail has been planned. There was a very good reason for him to speak to Officer Rabinowitz and only Rabinowitz. He did something he wanted her to see. He said something he wanted her to hear. But he did not want you," Noonan said to Agent Hastings, "to see it or hear it. What it was I do not know. But sooner or later, we'll figure it out."

Agent Hastings snagged the handkerchief inferior diamonds from Rabinowitz and turned to go but Noonan stopped him.

"If you don't mind, I'd like to take the diamonds George said were not authentic."

"Why? They have to go back to the command center." Agent Hastings had a puzzled look on his face.

"It's exactly what George wants us to do. To stay ahead of the game, we need to think ahead of him. George has said those diamonds were not authentic. I don't know if it's true. If you take the diamonds back to the command center it is going to take someone more than a day to examine the stones, then trace them back to the jeweler from when they came. I've got a better idea. Why don't we take them to a jeweler and ask for an appraisal?"

Agent Hastings looked at Noonan as if he were crazy.

"What? Why?"

"I don't know. All I do know is George expects us – no, wants us – to waste time taking them back to the command center."

"Even if that's true, I can't give you the diamonds on a whim. You aren't even official here."

"True, true," Noonan replied. Then he looked at Archie. "But Archie is with the Illinois State Troopers. He's official. Why don't the two of you take these to a reputable jeweler and see if these stones are authentic."

"Suppose they're not?" asked Archie.

"Then we're being played."

"I don't know about . . ." Agent Hastings started to say but Noonan politely cut him off.

"Agent Hastings. Nothing is going to happen here for about 24 hours. The command center is gathering diamonds and George is checking them. If you stay here, you'll just be standing around. Think of those stones," he pointed at the handkerchief bundle, "as a clue. You follow the clues where they lead."

Agent Hastings was clearly torn.

"Come on," Archie finally said. "It's a loose end. Let's follow it. There are more than enough jewelers in any one of the St. Louis malls. We can be there and back in about three hours. Nothing is going to happen in two or three hours."

Agent Hastings did not like the idea at all but it was not as if there was a Plan B to consider. With no reasonable choice, he relented. Before Agent Hasting and Archie left everyone exchanged cell phone numbers and then the two men were off. Noonan escorted the men as far as the door to the Mayor's Waiting Room. Rabinowitz started to get up but Noonan waved her back into her chair with his right hand, an arm and hand hidden from the sight of both Archie and Agent Hastings.

If they had turned around.

Which they did not.

As soon as the two men were gone, Noonan closed the door and sat down next to Rabinowitz.

"What was that all about?"

"My dear," said Noonan being avuncular, "what we have here is a plethora of distractions."

"A plethora?"

"Plethora, an overabundance. George and his gang are counting on confusion. That's why the bomb is in a bridge over the Mississippi River. Now two states and their bureaucracies are involved. Then there are the two cities, each on the shore of the river and two Homeland Security offices along with the FBI. There are five chains of command and very little coordination. It's what George wants: absolute confusion."

"Well, we need all of those people, all their expertise."

"Actually, we do NOT need all those people and their expertise. Those people are chasing all kinds of leads. Yes, over the long run, we will be able to put the entire picture together but by then George and his gang will be gone. With $50 million they can stay gone. What we have to do . . ."

"We?"

"You and I, officer, you and I."

"But I'm. . ."

"You are here. You've talked with George. George only wants to deal with you. You're in this up to your tonsils. You are now on the operational level whether you like it or not. Me, I'm a freelancer. I'm not in any chain of command, I don't have to follow any rules. You and I, Rabinowitz, we're the team. We didn't choose to be a team but here we are."

"But what about the other two, Agent . . .":

Noonan cut her off. "They are part of a command structure. We are not. They'll be back. But in the meantime, we must use our heads, not our feet."

"How do we do that?"

"First, you have to start thinking outside of the box. George snookered you. You just don't realize it yet. Let me tell you what you told me and then you tell me what I missed. You went into the room and George was seated at a desk covered with a black velvet spread."

"Correct."

"He had two piles of stones like small pyramids on both sides of him on a black velvet cloth that covered the desk."

"Yes."

"You saw him carefully scoop up some stones from a small pile and put them into a handkerchief."

"Yes."

"No you did not."

"Sorry."

"You did not see him see him scoop us some stones."

"Yes I did."

"No. I'm betting you were snookered. Think carefully, here's what I think happened. Agent Hastings left and George pointed to a small pile of diamonds next to a larger pyramid of diamonds. He said they were not authentic, scooped them up, put them in the handkerchief, tied the tags and handed you the bundle."

"That's right."

"Then he scooped another pile of supposedly authentic stones and put them in a little black bag."

"That's correct."

"No, that's not correct. You *believe* George scooped the authentic diamonds from the pyramid of diamonds. You did not actually see him do it. You were probably looking at the handkerchief when he supposedly scooped up the authentic diamonds. He only needed a split second when your attention was distracted. When you looked up, he had the diamonds in his palm. You assumed they had come from a pile of diamonds he had been examining."

"They were!"

"Maybe. Maybe not. But what George wants you to think is the authentic diamonds are in little black bags in his briefcase."

"They are."

"Maybe. Maybe not."

"Even if they are not, what difference does it make? Why all the buzz about the fake diamonds? Who cares? We've got them and we'll sort them out. Even if George is long gone we'll know who handed in the phonies."

Noonan smiled like a Dutch uncle. "First, the diamonds he put in the handkerchief are most likely ringers. But those diamonds most likely were not collected from any jeweler. George had them all along. See, all expensive stones have fingerprints."

"I know that. That's how we can trace stolen stones."

"True. But if the diamonds George gave us were not collected from local jewelers . . ."

Rabinowitz cut him off, "It will take us a year and a day to find out."

"You are catching on quickly. Now follow George's thinking. If he says certain stones are not authentic, who does he give the stones to?"

"Oh, I don't know. Maybe the person who brought him the stones in the first place."

"No. Overall this is a federal operation because the bomb is over the Mississippi River. Technically the FBI is in charge."

"Agent Hastings?"

"George was counting on the FBI being involved and he guessed – correctly – the FBI would send in Agent Hastings. It was a natural. He's dealt with Agent Hastings before. The FBI sends in their best so it would send Agent Hastings. George knows Agent Hastings is coming so he develops some ways to sideline him."

"How did he do that?"

"By putting fake diamonds in a handkerchief. This bundle George gave you is called evidence and the FBI has strict rules about how evidence is handled. The FBI has a chain of custody when it comes to evidence. An agent cannot just give evidence to someone else in law enforcement. George gave you evidence in a federal case and Agent Hastings took the evidence. Agent Hastings now must follow the rules of evidence. In this case, because time is short, he cannot take the evidence to the local FBI office. He has to run with it. I'm betting he is calling the lab people to meet him at some jeweler where they will take the handkerchief and inventory the diamonds before they let any jeweler touch the stones."

"So that was George's way of sidelining Agent Hastings."

"You are catching on fast!"

"So if the diamonds in the handkerchief are fake and it will take hours to find out they are fake. In the meantime, Agent Hastings is tied up in FBI paperwork."

"Oh, he's not a stupid man. He will figure it out quickly and he'll be back. But, for the moment, George wants him gone. Out of the picture."

"Why?"

"That, my dear lady, I do not know."

East St. Louis
Saturday, July 3rd
High   88°
Low   71°
Precipitation: 0
Humidity: 54%
Wind: 7 mph

CHAPTER 28

It took a little over 30 hours to find the hostages. The full-scale publicity blitz by the Joint
Homeland Security Commission for Missouri and Illinois paid off handsomely. Local television stations cut into regular programming with a call for help. Every community with an inch of a spur track between St. Louis and Chicago joined in the search. Within three hours the locomotive was located. It was in plain sight and the reason it had not been spotted before was because it was not alone on a spur track. The terrorists, the term used by the – Italicized and bold – ***JOINT HOME-LAND SECURITY COMMISSION*** – and beneath the lettering was the listing of three states – as stated on its stationery still wet from the printer – had left the locomotive in queue behind two others. The only way the locomotive would have been discovered was for a locomotive by locomotive search up and down and the rail line. That was exactly what had happened and the ***JOINT HOMELAND SECURITY COMMIS-SION*** announced the locomotive had been found at an undisclosed location – to confuse the terrorists – and now the hunt was on for hostages.

The search for the hostages proved a lot easier. There were not too many places within a 30-minute bus ride from the rail lines where 70 people could be held hostage without being seen. Once the overflights left the rail line it was not long before a massive smoke plume was spotted on the grounds of an abandoned nuclear missile site. The local fire department was called and the hostages were discovered. The abandoned buses were discovered shortly thereafter in an abandoned barn five miles from where the locomotive was located.

Suddenly it was a publicity footrace between the **JOINT HOME-LAND SECURITY COMMISSION**, the fire department which had found the hostages and the hostages themselves. No one could keep anyone quiet. The press, desperate to fill the 24-hour news cycle and, in the case of newspapers, sell print copies, were on the story even as the hostages were in transit to St. Louis – Missouri, not Illinois. The hostages were trading their rescuers cell phones around and making calls to spouses, relatives and press outlets even as the rescue buses were moving. This precipitated a flood of calls, visits and on-camera interviews with relatives which were broadcast across the United States. The hostages were rock stars before they arrived in St. Louis. The hour and a half trip to St. Louis allowed just enough time for everyone with an inkling of interest to meet-and-greet the homegoing celebrities. The original plan was to drop them inside the St. Louis train terminal but so many people showed up to greet them their announced destination it had to be changed to the sparsely-filled long-term parking lot. The Auxiliary Exit was opened so the three-bus convoy could enter, drop off its passengers to a hero's welcome and then exit the parking lot the same way it entered.

This created a massive public relations problem for the **JOINT HOMELAND SECURITY COMMISSION.** Now the Commission had to explain why the terrorists had not been caught, where those terrorists might be and, at the same time, not mention a word about a massive explosive device in the most-used bridge crossing the Mississippi between St. Louis and the "rest of the civilized" world as radio station KWTR called the East Coast. The commissioners rose to the occasion and nominated Commissioner Lizzard as the spokesman for the group. This was an incredibly ingenious move as it made explaining why North Carolina was involved in a matter only affecting Illinois and Missouri, states which did not border North Carolina. Lizzard stated it was all hush-hush for the moment and, at the proper time, a full accounting would be made. As to any details, Lizzard lamented the FBI was in charge of the investigation and all questions should be addressed to its office.

This was quadruply clever. First, because the FBI never discusses cases it may or may not be investigating. Second, it effectively blocked any questions which may or may not have been asked about the sudden, supposedly secret but becoming well-known collection of diamonds from jewelry stores in the two cities of St. Louis, and the boxcar blocking the rail line inside the Eads Bridge. Third, it gave the *JOINT HOME-LAND SECURITY COMMISSION* cover to ask for immediate federal money for the "ongoing matter over the Mississippi River" to resolve this "case of domestic terrorism."

Fourth and most important, Commissioner Lizzard was from North Carolina. The local press and television stations had inside sources with the Illinois and Missouri law enforcement office but when it came to North Carolina they had zip. Even if a newspaper reporter had could reach the Governor of North Carolina, no one on the Governor's executive staff would have known anything about Lizzard or what he was doing in either St. Louis.

Statements by the *JOINT HOMELAND SECURITY COMMIS-SION* mollified the press for the moment – but only for the moment. Unfortunately for the law enforcement there were a lot of questions it could not answer. Worse, even if there was an answer, law enforcement was loathed to respond. Chief among these questions was why? Why go to the effort of taking hostages in the first place and not demand ransom? The hostages had not been guarded, why not? If the hostages were expected to be rescued so soon, why go to the effort at all? Then there was the train. There were a lot easier ways to take hostages so why go to the effort of hijacking a train? And even if the *JOINT HOME-LAND SECURITY COMMISSION* had stopped a domestic terrorist incident, what happened to the terrorists? Had they simply vanished into the ether? Or had they gone to ground? Were they waiting for another chance at a senseless crime? Exactly what was going on here?

It did not take long for the press to pick up the proverbial 'rest of the story.' The *East St. Louis Gazetteer* was the first to scoop the truth and printed photos of the inside of the Command Center. No one in East St. Louis believed the paper because, after all, it *was* the *East St. Louis Gazetteer*, a grocery store tabloid which gave the *National Enquirer* a run for the local money. It was not until a local television station ran clandestine footage of the Command Center did responsible news junkies take notice. Then the cat was out of the bag. Suddenly everyone took notice of the solitary boxcar sitting along on the track under the car and truck traffic lanes on the Eads Bridge.

When the news of the jewelry stores being ransacked for diamonds became general press knowledge, it did not take a rocket science to piece the story together. Within hours the Eads Bridge was closed off to foot traffic on both sides of the Mississippi River.

All this said there was a rather deleterious downside to the hostage resolution. Suddenly, with less than two dozen hours to go before a bomb was to detonate in the Eads Bridge, it allowed the full force of all law enforcement offices of both the states of Missouri and Illinois to concentrate on the only problem left.

The only saving grace was law enforcement did not have to worry about sequestering the boxcar. It was on a railroad track in the center of the bridge beneath the car and truck traffic lanes. The rail lines onto and off the bridge were barricaded and the roadway was closed off on both sides of the river. A handful of surplus combat vehicles were parked at irregular intervals and angles on the bridge roadway to stall any attempt at landing any aircraft. Water launches, courtesy of the United States Coast Guard, were patrolling the water below. There was also a collection of Navy SEALS available just in case they were needed for underwater security.

Had this been the extent of the obstructions it would have been sufficient. There were other bridges which crossed the Mississippi. This meant the traffic was inconvenienced but not stopped. But what made the situation intolerable were the thousands of looky-loos now crowding the riverbanks. Both sides. Something was going to happen and they, one and all, wanted to be there when it happened. To be part of history.

The catchphrase for the day, repeatedly stated by Commissioner Lizzard and picked by the press, was "hidden in plain sight." Lizzard was particularly pleased to see it associated with his name. In headlines: "HOSTAGES HIDDEN IN PLAIN SIGHT' says Commissioner Lizzard." Rapidly thereafter the term was used to describe how the errant locomotive had been "hidden in plain sight," the buses which had spirited the hostages away were "hidden in plain sight," and, finally, the railway car in the Eads Bridge was "hidden in plain sight."

However, there was a poisonous development to the use of the term. Because everything associated with this "developing terrorist attack" was "hidden in plain sight," every aspect of the "developing terrorist attack" was in public view. The press loved it! Now, instead of on-camera talking heads using hand-held pointers on maps of both cities of St. Louis, there were live interviews from both banks of the Mississippi River, ongoing comments from the three commissioners of the *JOINT HOMELAND SECURITY COMMISSION* , interviews with city officials from both cities of St. Louis – and all on a usually v-e-r-y slow weekend where the biggest news previous years had been hot dog eating contest winners and fireworks displays. It turned the three-day weekend into a carnival with looky-loos following the press coverage.

While the commissioners were not concerned with the intense press coverage, bottom rank and file law and order personnel from both cities and the federal agencies which had on the ground operatives were collectively holding their breaths. Media coverage means crowds and large numbers of people can panic easily. Anything can set off a crowd of looky-loos.

Anything.

CHAPTER 29

Justice, Defense and Homeland Security had no problem meeting in public. It was actually safer that way. Not that they were doing anything clandestine. No more than any other collection of highly-placed civil servants. They were doing what all civil servants do, regardless of paygrade or Department: preserving their jobs.

A little interdepartmental help every now and again was a good idea. For them specifically.

Homeland Security assured the others things on and off the bridge were just fine.

Justice tapped a cigarette on the park bench. "The beef is going from this burger. What we've got now is a negotiation. We have an agent on the ground and that's as far as we're willing to go." Justice raised his eyes skyward when he used the pronoun *we*. "The prevailing feeling is this has bad news written all over it. *We*," again the eyes skyward, "do not see an upside at this point. If the bridge goes, *we* do not want to be seen as being anywhere near the trigger. If this man gets away, *we* don't want to be seen as being negligent. There's an FBI agent on the ground, retired, and if things go south, he'll take the heat. We want to come out of the water dry and this is our moment to get out of the pool."

Defense nodded. "It's *our* position as well. We don't see one more vote moving *our* way because of this matter, whichever way it goes." Defense emphasized the words *one more vote*. "There is no percentage here. We've made the commitment to cover the back door. Now there is no back door. There is no role for Defense here."

Homeland Security had no problem with the abandonment of the ship. "Our people figured this was going to be the case. We've got three people on the ground. What I would suggest," Homeland Security specifically looked at Justice, "is the FBI agent on site be specifically told he takes his orders from Homeland Security. It will give us on-ground control on-site."

Justice smiled. "We don't see a problem. In fact, it's an excellent idea. It removes us back one more step. I'll make sure the agent understands he is to take his instruction and guidance Homeland Security."

"That leaves you the only team in the ballpark," Defense said to Homeland Security. "This has all the earmarks of a disaster." There was silence for a moment and Defense continued. "Get all your good people out of the line of fire. Leave the garbage." There was a long pause and Defense looked sideways at Homeland Security. "Your people could muck this up."

"Oh, they will. We know that." Homeland Security smiled. "See, we are counting on it. Right now, we have three men in the field, far too few to handle an emergency case like this. Success simply means we have enough men and mater-i-el to handle all manner of problems in the area. Failure can be profitable," he smiled. "We," he said as he looked upwards, "do not see a downside with regard to failure."

CHAPTER 30

There was only one word to describe the twin banks of the Mississippi River at the Eads Bridge: carnival. It was the best show in town. Both of them. From the instant the newspaper-reading public put two and two together – the disappearing diamonds and the stranded box car – they clogged the riverbanks. This was easy because local law enforcement had closed the bridge to vehicular traffic which, in effect, left it wide open for foot traffic.

If it is open, they will come.

And come they did.

For selfies and with television cameras. The crowd overwhelmed the few police on both ends of the bridge and swarmed onto the boxcar like ants on a deer carcass. It was not a crowd; it was a carpet. It took the locals a good four hours to restore order and move the crowd back from the boxcar and onto the riverbanks.

Both governors put in calls for the National Guard but it would take a full 24 hours for the Guard to be operationally strong. So, in the meantime, guard duty was left to the local police, troopers and highway patrol from both states. They could reach the bridge in a matter of hours and they did. When order was restored the bridge looked to be carpeted with blue and black uniforms replacing the motley fabric of the crowds of looky-loos.

The Eads Bridge was the focus of not only the two states but the world as well. Everyone with a computer or television was watching the 24/7 drama as it was unfolding. This was particularly true of the locals who expected, at any moment, to see the century-old structure leap skyward and vaporize into a shower of century and a half old bricks, mortar and steel. There were so many officers on and around the bridge it was laughingly said if the bridge went, it would take another century and a half before the local police forces would be back to full strength.

This concentration of police on the Eads Bridge created a dearth of police on the street. This was not a long-term problem because it was a three-day holiday and many businesses were closed. But it was a difficulty faced by the tourist attractions and special events. These were geared up to take advantage of the three-day holiday. Restaurants were packed, museums were open and theme parks had extended hours. The "Game of the Century" between the St. Louis Cardinals and Denver Rockies made public it was delaying the transfer of any moneys from the stadium to the banks because of the shortage of support law enforcement and the banks which remained open hired armored car staff to double as security guards. The few planned armored car runs within both cities were canceled and retired police officers were lured back to duty to handle 911 calls. This crisis was only going to last another 24 hours but it was going to be a very turbulent 24 hours with everyone waiting to see what was going to happen next.

Then someone in the press discovered George was going over the diamonds one at a time in the East St. Louis City Hall. This tidbit moved a large contingent of the crowd off the riverbank and into East St. Louis. That was the good news. The bad news was that the crowd surrounded the East St. Louis City Hall.

Worse news was the clock kept ticking.

CHAPTER 31

"What are we going to do now?" Commissioner Lizzard was commiserating with the other joint commissioners. What had started as a golden opportunity of fun, friends and funding had ended in a choice of flame or flood. The terrorist storyline still held because the hostages kept talking to the media about *terrorists* dressed camouflage and wearing ski masks and no press person had made the solid leap from hostages to the bomb in the Eads Bridge.

Yet.

There might not have been. After all, there was no solid link. But it did not take a rocket scientist to make the link. But, now, there was no solid link between the two. It was the only saving grace. When it was finally discovered the two were connected, it was probably going to be too late to would make no difference.

George was another matter altogether. At the moment, he had received about $8 million in stones but the going had been slow. It had taken almost 24 hours to start the gathering of the diamonds and only after the stones had been gathered could they be inventoried and cataloged. It was a horribly time-consuming task and the diamonds going to George were in batches. It had been neither reasonable nor possible to save the stones until the threshold of $10 million was reached and then dump all the stones on his table. To speed up the process, the stones had been given to him smaller amounts. He had not complained. Then again, since the hostages had been released there was no longer a timetable for the initial millions.

But still, time was running out for the bridge.

Which is what worried Lizzard and the other commissioners.

"Gentlemen," Lizzard said below his breath, "we have a real problem. We've got a bomb timed to go off in a dozen hours and this George fellow still needs millions more in diamonds. We don't have any accurate accounting of how much he has received but we are not anywhere near the $50 million mark. Even if we move as fast as we can we are still not going to make his deadline."

Mustafa Sanchez shook his head. "We are in this up to our elbows and it is starting to fall apart. What if we don't give this George guy what he wants the bridge goes and we look bad. If we give him what he wants and he gets away, we look bad."

"We can always hope someone will catch him," said Boris Yang. "It will give us an out."

The other two looked at him as if he were crazy. "Boris," snapped Lizzard, "we want to look good whatever does happen. If someone else catches him, we'll look bad too. It was something WE should have done. It was something WE should have prepared for. What we need to do is cover ourselves if things go south."

"So you are saying someone has to take the blame?" The tone of Boris' voice indicated he didn't not have a problem at all with this.

"Not blame, Boris," snapped Sanchez. "*Responsibility*. Someone must be assigned to this matter who will take the *responsibility*. If he succeeds we take the credit. If he fails, he takes the blame. Either way we come out ahead."

"Well, we'd better be really careful, guys, because the guy who ends up with egg on his face can't be working for any of us. That pretty much rules out everyone involved. There are no free-floating individuals." Yang scratched his head.

"Not really," said Sanchez very carefully. "There is the retired FBI guy, what's his name?"

"Who cares? Naw, it won't work. He's FBI. Besides, we will need the FBI. Don't muddy the waters where you want to drink. We should pull Yenokovian out of the command structure immediately. He's a rising star we cannot afford to lose. That woman, whatever her name is, she can stay. She can go down with the ship. She's expendable. We don't need people, women, like her on the force anyway. Then there's that Noonan fellow. Lizzard, what's his first name?"

"Heinz. But I've got to work with him. I'm not sure. . ."

Yang cut in. "Lizzard, think of it this way. It won't make any different to anyone in North Carolina what went down in St. Louis. But it will make a very big difference here, to us." He pointed from himself to Sanchez. "We will still be here when you go home," he said pointing at Lizzard.

"But it leaves me with egg on my face," sulked Lizzard.

"Maybe not," said Yang looking at Sanchez. "The Joint Commission has a lot of emergency moneys. We could get a lot more money to study what we *didn't do that we could have done.*"

"So what you are saying is we could make a lot more money for the Joint Commission if we fail?" Lizzard shook his head as if to clear cobwebs. "That doesn't make sense."

Suddenly it did.

A lot of sense.

Dollars too.

CHAPTER 32

The Mayor of East St. Louis was roasting marshmallows over a campfire in the Adirondacks when he got the news. He and his family had purposely left their cell phones in East St. Louis. This was to be a bonding three-day weekend. It was only in conversation with a fellow hiker who did have a cell phone that the Mayor learned of the hijacking of the train. By the time he reached his staff, George was already in the building.

There was no way the Mayor could reach East St. Louis before the end of the 48-hour time clock so he did not try. He simply contacted the Deputy Mayor and ordered her to clear the building of all municipal staff – of which there were none because it was a three-day holiday – and work with law enforcement of both cities and both states – until he returned. He also ordered her to prepare two sets of press releases. One if the events culminated in a success and the other, just in case, things went south.

Before the battery on the cell phone died, the Mayor ordered the Deputy Mayor to backstop the police and make sure there was no way this George fellow could slip out of City Hall with the diamonds unnoticed. "You know," he said, "like in one of the Bourne movies where Matthew Bourne sets off a fire alarm and then slips out of the building dressed as a fireman. And make sure there's no way this George fellow can drop the diamonds out of the window to someone in a back alley, hand glide into the next block or use an old railway tunnel under City Hall. This is, is, is bizarre, let me tell you. I didn't get elected to deal with actual terrorists, only public utility managers who act like terrorists."

CHAPTER 33

Rabinowitz was giving an update at the Command Center when Agent Hastings and Archie made it back from the jeweler.

"Let me guess," said Noonan before Agent Hastings could begin speaking. "The diamonds are inferior but not flawed or fake. They are just run-of-the-mill, not big dollar."

"You read us like a book," Archie said. "Not fake. Not flawed. Inferior, yes. But not cut glass or costume jewelry."

Agent Hastings cut in. "A wild good chase."

"Absolutely," Noonan said as he took the bag from Agent Hastings. "George wanted you to be out of the picture for a while. My bet? He considers you the most dangerous of the lot."

"He only knows me. Archie and Rabinowitz are new to him." Agent Hastings tone was flat and professional.

"I doubt it. He's planned too well to take any chances. He may not know them intimately, the way he does you, but he has a good idea how they operate. George wants to make sure he's dealing with line cops like Archie and Rabinowitz. He can play them like a violin – not so much you."

"He doesn't know you," Archie said to Noonan. "That could be our ace in the hole."

"Don't bet on that. He has a computer with access to the internet. I'll bet the moment the Joint Homeland Security taskforce was announced he tracked Lizzard to Sandersonville and then pulled up our cases. If he didn't know who I was six hours ago, he knows now."

"Well maybe you should say 'hello,'" suggested Archie. "Let's throw a monkey wrench into his plans." He was about to continue speaking when his cell phone buzzed. He held up the index finger of his right hand and said, "I've got to take this. It's official."

Archie stepped aside and Noonan took the bag of diamonds from Agent Hastings. He held it up in front of Agent Hastings face.

"George gave Rabinowitz these diamonds in a handkerchief, didn't he?"

"Yes."

"Then where did you get this bag?"

"At the jeweler's. It's an institutional bag. All the jewelry dealers have them."

"Same color? Same size?"

"W-e-l-l no. I saw some blue and green ones and some were bigger."

"How about the bags George had?

"I wasn't there long enough to see any. Ask Rabinowitz."

"OK." Noonan tossed the bag gently in his hand.

"Careful," said Agent Hastings. That's evidence."

"Actually, I don't think so. I'm betting these are ringers. Diamonds George came with. When they are eventually checked, I'm betting we'll find they weren't part of the looted diamonds. Just another way to misdirect us, taking time away from what is important."

"Maybe so. But it's still evidence by the book."

"Well, let's not take these anywhere just yet." Noonan said jiggling the bag. "I'm suggesting we keep these diamonds here. If we take it down to the Command Center we are going to have an hour's worth of paperwork. We leave them here. They are still under our control. We cannot do what George wants us to do."

Before Agent Hastings could respond, Archie cut the phone call short.

"Sorry to tell you I've been reassigned," Archie said. "I'm to coordinate with the engineer of the hijacked train. Right now." He stuck his hand out to Agent Hastings and Noonan. "I really, really, wanted to be in on this one." He tapped his phone with his index finger. "But I'm needed elsewhere. I hope it's as exciting there as this has been!"

"Pleasure working with you, Archie." Agent Hastings smiled and shook his hand.

Noonan shook Archie's hand and walked Archie to the door.

After Archie had left, Agent Hastings looked at Noonan and the message was clear as crystal.

"We're being hung out to dry." Agent Hastings shook his head.

"You knew it was going to happen sooner or later," Noonan said. "It's a good bet they want Rabinowitz to go down with the ship."

CHAPTER 34

"Where's Archie?" Rabinowitz looked behind Agent Hastings as she came through the door of the Mayor's Waiting Room. "He left with you."

"He got called to duty by a higher authority."

"His wife?" Rabinowitz asked.

"Fun-ny lady," said Agent Hastings with a wry smile. It was the first time Noonan had seen him crack his lips. "No. He's been assigned to work with the engineer from the train. They're covering the back tracks."

"That's odd." Rabinowitz looked at Noonan sideways. "What does the engineer of a hijacked train have to do with a boxcar in a bridge?"

Noonan looked at Agent Hastings and Agent Hastings looked at Noonan and they both looked at Rabinowitz.

"What?" snapped Rabinowitz. "Are we keeping secrets?"

"Rabinowitz," Noonan was slow and measured. "You have a lot to learn about the real world. Right now, no one knows what to do. Everyone is anticipating failure and no one wants to be blamed when things go wrong."

"Things go wrong?" Rabinowitz was irate. "How can things go wrong? The hostages are free, the train has been recovered, we've got George surrounded in a building. What's going to go wrong?"

"Rabinowitz," Agent Hastings was slow and deliberate. "We are the sacrificial lambs. If things go well, we will get a pat on the back and everyone above us will get a medal. If things go wrong, we get the blame. It's easy. See, I'm retired. There is nothing anyone can do to me. This case will just be the one I could not bring to a successful conclusion. You can't win them all."

"I'm past retirement," said Noonan. "If I must retire, that's the way the ball bounces. I'll miss the chase but I've got a home on the beach and a phone. I don't need to work. But you," he said pointing at Rabinowitz, "are the one who is being set up for the fall. I'm betting you're not too popular with the folks in your department."

"Boy, have you got that right," snapped Rabinowitz. "I'm looking to get out but nothing is breaking my way."

"What he's saying," interjected Agent Hastings, "is everyone thinks we're going to fail. They do not see success here. So, they are covering their butts early. They are not going to be the fall guys when things go bad – and they believe that things are going to go very badly."

"They don't just think it," Noonan cut in. "They're counting on it. In this business, there's more glory in losing than winning. The crime rate goes up, there's more money for law enforcement. It's a fact of life."

"So we're getting hung out to dry?" Rabinowitz was not clearly not pleased.

"You are being treated like God," said Agent Hastings with a straight face.

Rabinowitz kind of shook her head to clear her thoughts. "Like God? Where did, did?" she could not finish the line.

"It's an old joke, officer. The punch line is no one believes in you until they need you. Right now, no one needs us. We will be pariahs until . . ."

"Until we are needed, right?" Rabinowitz finished his sentence.

"Fraid so." Noonan was bright. "But, you see, there is a very bright side."

"Really," Rabinowitz was still assessing what was happening to her career. "If there is, I don't see it."

"Rabinowitz, take a seat." Noonan pointed to four chairs at a round table. Agent Hastings and Noonan took seats opposite Rabinowitz. "Rabinowitz, you are thinking like a regular cop. Punch in, chase bad people, arrest bad people, clock out. Regular job. This is not regular gig."

"You can say that again."

"I would but time is of the essence. See, all the people who want us to fail have no idea what to do. They are punch-in-clock-out people. What they see is a clever guy who's probably going to get $50 million in diamonds and skip town. They don't know how to stop him because they do not think like he does. Their minds cannot grasp the fact George is not a grab-and-dash diamond thief. Since they cannot think like George, they just assume he is going to get away."

Agent Hastings cut it. "So they are covering their bets. If he doesn't get away, they get the laurels. If he does, we get the blame. At this point they don't see how he is going to get away but they need a back-up plan."

"That's us, right?"

"Yup, Rabinowitz, it's us. We are the fail-safe." Noonan smiled. "But the big boys up the food chain are making one big mistake. They are assuming we will fail."

"Rather, because they are hoping we will fail," cut in Agent Hastings. "They are going to give us a free hand. They are going to cut us free."

"Rabinowitz, this is your moment to shine. Any time now you'll get a call from your commander who will tell you to hang close to the FBI. To play along with the FBI. They won't tell you to report back, just assist the FBI."

"I've already been told that."

Noonan looked at Agent Hastings and they both nodded knowingly.

"Now here's the rest of the good news," Noonan smiled and leaned forward. "George is unlikely to get away with it. He and his crew have planned for every contingent possibility. So far they have been spot on. That's because they are dealing with cops who think like cops and bureaucrats who think like bureaucrats."

"But we don't think that way," Agent Hastings cut in. "So we have an edge. We can beat this guy. It'll take a little bit of luck, yes, but we can beat this guy."

"It doesn't look so good from where I'm sitting."

"OK," Noonan cut in. "Let's be creative. Let's say George gets his diamonds, then what?"

"I haven't thought that far ahead."

"Then start," snapped Agent Hastings. "You are in a whole new ball game, Rabinowitz. See, George is not going to get the last load of diamonds unless he disables the bomb and he is not going to disable the bomb without the diamonds."

"How is that going to work out?"

"That, officer Rabinowitz, is what divides the boys from the men or, in your case, the girls from the commanders."

"So we have to start thinking ahead of game."

"Now you're getting it," said Noonan happily. "In the meantime, let's see if we can upset George's applecart. But first I've got a couple of questions for you."

"OK. Shoot."

"George handed you the diamonds in a handkerchief, correct?"

"Yes. He said they were inferior. Were they?"

"Not really," cut in Agent Hastings. "Average as opposed to excellent."

"Huh" said Rabinowitz as she looked at Noonan, her eyes asking for an explanation.

"Everything is important. Now the diamonds are in the small pile in front of George. You saw him put them in a little bag, correct?"

"Yes. A small black one."

"Like this one?" Noonan held up the black jeweler's bag Agent Hastings had picked up in the jewelry store.

"Well, for texture and color, yes. But the bags George has are bigger. The ones I am transporting the diamond to him are bigger too. Palm size."

"Black?"

"Jet black."

"When you saw the pile of bags. . ."

"I didn't see a pile of bags. He put diamonds in a bag," she pointed to the bag in Noonan's hand. "Then he put the bag in a briefcase beside him." She pointed to the little bag in Noonan's hand. "That's a small bag. The ones I am bringing up from the diamond desk are the same texture and color but larger. Like I said, palm-size. Is it important?"

"At this point. Everything is important."

CHAPTER 35

Heinz Noonan! The bearded Holmes. You make your appearance at last!"

Noonan was not at all surprised that George knew who he was. "I see you have been doing your homework."

George looked exactly as Rabinowitz had described him. The only thing Noonan noticed that Rabinowitz did not mention was that George sat oddly. As if he had a slight injury to one side of his body.

"Ah, the 24-hour news cycle and the internet are a gift of the gods to men like me." George smiled.

"I note you did not say God in the singular."

"Mr. Noonan! For shame! I am of the material world. I have damaged no one. I'm simply taking from those who have it to lose: insurance companies. At the end of the day they will pay and as long as everyone plays by my rules, no one will get hurt."

"That's a heck of a risk, George. Can I call you George?"

"Certainly! And I'll call you Heinz. I have been expecting you."

"I'll take that as a compliment. Now, as you know, there are a lot of moving parts in this matter of yours. You know no matter how fast we move we will not be able to get you $50 million in diamonds before your timetable runs out."

"That would be most unfortunate," George shook his head sadly. "I was anticipating the collection would go faster. But then again," he smiled. "What can you expect of a bureaucracy? I will expect the entire $50 million before this matter is over."

Noonan leaned back against the door frame. "I'm not going to give you the tired line of 'you can't get away with this' but I would suggest you start thinking about a Plan B. Right now there is no way to get $50 million in diamonds to you in the time we have left. This means you will have either take what you have and leave or reset the bomb. Can the bomb be reset?"

"Can the bomb be reset? An interesting way of phrasing it. Yes, the clockwork can be restarted but not reset. You see, anticipating restart after restart, the bomb has been programmed for one restart if necessary. Only one. But once the restart is initiated, it only lasts for 24 additional hours and then things go boom."

"You phrase it so delicately," Noonan said. "There's going to be a lot of damage and loss of life when, to use your term, 'things go boom.' Then you will be out of options."

"True, true. But I do not anticipate that, to paraphrase myself, 'thing will go boom.'"

Noonan stroked his beard. "George, let's be serious now. There is no way you are going to get $50 million in the time you have set out. I doubt you will get the whole $50 million even if you reset the explosive device. So, before we get down to the wire on the 20 odd hours we have left, let's talk about the next step. What are you going to do when there are only a few hours left on the 48 hours?"

George smiled. "I anticipated the police would try to move as slowly as possible. That's an unfortunate reality of dealing with the police. What I have here," he waved his hand over a pile of small velvet black bags and a small pile of diamonds, "is about $10 to $15 million. Individual diamonds do not have a set value. But you are correct. We are going to miss the first deadline."

"It was a bogus deadline, George. And you know it. You knew we were going to find the hostages fairly quickly. You didn't put any guards on the abandoned sanitarium. I am guessing the hostages were simply a distraction."

George smiled. "Ah, you live up to your reputation. Searching for the hostages cut the police force in both cities of St. Louis by half. It was cut in half again when they had to go after the diamonds. An entire police force can be quite efficient. But if they are scattered in assignment and geography, well, it leaves an opening for a man like me."

"You are playing a very dangerous game, George. If something goes wrong the bridge and a lot of innocent people are going to die. Then, no matter where you go, we can bring you back."

"Heinz! No one is going to get hurt! We are a good eight hours out from things going boom. So, let's come up with a Plan B. Let's see where we are four hours from now. If you show good faith on your side by keeping up the flow of diamonds, I'll reset the timer. But like I told you, I can only do it once."

"Well, at least it will give us another 24 hours," Noonan said.

"Don't play me for a fool, Heinz. I'll only play ball as long as we're both honest with each other."

"That's odd coming from you."

"What? Being a compromiser?"

"No. Using the term *honest*."

CHAPTER 36

The three commissioners drew straws to see in what order they, individually, would speak to the press. But this was not a usual game of short straw. It was for who talked with the press when. There were three of them so, perforce, there were going to be three press conferences. One each. Each of them would get their moment to shine. *Publicity* was what a Joint Commission was all about. *Joint* as in three as one and one as three. It was the glue holding them together. Rather, it was the glue which would allow all of them – individually – to request the funding to continue their exemplary teamwork – in three different locales.

Win, lose or draw they would be able to cross the United States seminar by conference by convention. *How we faced down the terrorist and won. How we faced the greatest crisis in our state's history and defeated the terrorist.* Why there might even be a book deal at the end of the saga. God had surely come down on earth and blessed them, one-two-three, Lizzard, Yang and Sanchez.

There was certainly money in failure.

If you did it right.

They planned to do it right.

It was Lizzard first.

The make-shift press room in the ballroom of the Bond Hotel on 10th Avenue was jammed to the walls. There was a bank of cameras peering over the heads of the press people and Lizzard could barely be seen over the podium which had microphone clusters like barnacles on a pier pillar. Lizzard stepped up on a stool to make him appear taller and gave a chamber of commerce smile before he sank into seriousness.

(No one could ever say his years at Toastmaster were wasted!)

He cleared his throat for emphasis and to quiet the hubbub.

"First, the Joint Homeland Security Commission for Missouri, North Carolina and Illinois is pleased you are here today. As you know we are in the middle of a terrorist crisis" he said emphasizing the word *terrorist*. "I will try to be as forthcoming as possible with what we know at this moment."

He took a prepared pause followed by a deep breath, both calculated to emphasis he was in charge.

"As We Speak and, as you know, diamonds are being collected from jewelers in both St. Louis cities. A man known only to us by the name George is examining the diamonds in the East St. Louis City Hall. When he has the entire $50 million he will give us the code for the explosive device in the boxcar in the Eads Bridge. We, that is, the Joint Homeland Security Commission, believe it is the best interest of the local and state governments to pay the money rather than see the bridge destroyed."

There was a buzz in the press of the press with questions being shouted from the gallery. Lizzard held up his hands, prophet-like and waved them to silence the crowd.

"Anticipating your questions, let me generally respond. First, we do not know how this George is going to make his escape. We also do not yet know how the final exchange is going to be made. We will not give him the last collection of diamonds unless we have disarmed the explosive device and he will not disarm the explosive device without the diamonds. This is a sticking point we have not yet resolved."

Lizzard took a breath and went on before the deluge of questions could begin again.

"We are taking every precaution to make sure this caper comes to a satisfying end. As you know we have sealed off the Eads Bridge on both sides. The railway is blocked and there are military assault vehicles in place on the railway and on the bridge. George is currently in the East St. Louis City Hall and we have the building surrounded. We have also placed men on the roof of City Hall to make certain George does not attempt an escape by air. Three contingent of Navy SEALS are onboard a combat Zodiac in the Mississippi River to stop any attempt by George to escape by water. The United States Air Force also has several jets available just in case they are needed. I am not familiar with the type of aircraft the United States Air Force has made available but I have been assured whether George leaves by jet, helicopter, ultralight or on fairy wings, he will be followed. That's all I can tell you now and I would be pleased to answer any questions you may have," he paused, "if the answer does not compromise national security."

CHAPTER 37

President of the United States

White House
1600 Pennsylvania Avenue NW
Washington, D.C. 20500

F OR IMMEDIATE RELEASE:
    July 3

"As many of you know we are in the midst of an act of terrorism on the Eads Bridge which connects St. Louis, Missouri and East St. Louis, Illinois across the Mississippi River. I have ordered the Department of Homeland Security to act as the lead with support from the Department of Justice and the Federal Bureau of Investigation. As an explosive device is involved, I have ordered the Combat Engineers from Fort Leonard Wood to be on-site and available to the Department of Homeland Security.

For the moment, the Eads Bridge across the Mississippi River is closed to all traffic and a protective perimeter has been extended on both sides of the river. While this is causing traffic difficulties, let me assure all residents of Missouri and Illinois, this is only a temporary situation.

Also at the present time, the Department of Homeland Security is in communication with the terrorists. The Department of Homeland Security will be providing real-time updates throughout the day. Please be assured this is a matter of the highest national priority and the American people can rest assured every available military and civilian unit is being called upon to resolve this issue. The Joint Homeland Security Commission in East St. Louis is spearheading this effort and it is in touch with this office on an hourly schedule.

Thank you very much and God Bless the United States of America.

CHAPTER 38

When things click, the devil will have his due. Prior to the Lizzard press conference, the public was juggling circumstances. That is, they, individually and collectively, had a myriad of jigsaw puzzle pieces with no clear picture of what the picture would look like when the pieces were assembled. Everyone could see the pieces in play but not place them in any kind of a composite picture. There had been the hijacking of three dome cars to the north along with the disappearance of the FAM reporters and the crew of the train. Then there was the collection of diamonds from jewelers in both cities of St. Louis along with an isolated boxcar in the Eads Bridge which supposedly housed an "explosive device" of unknown strength. But there had been no coherent thread linking all of them to a single cause. In the mind of the public it was like four murders taking place in the same city over the same weekend. The public would know of each of the murders but could not logically leap to the conclusion there was a serial killer at large. Four murders in a single weekend just meant you lived in a violent city. And in south St. Louis – both of them – well, wasn't that par for the course? But if the four murders were linked it meant you had a serial killer on the loose. Now everyone – uptown, downtown, all around the town – would be locking their windows and doors and checking with friends and neighbors hourly. No one knew who was going to be next.

The press conference hosted by Commissioner Lizzard identified George as the nexus of all the disparate parts of the puzzle. Then came the click of connection. Instantaneously disparate facts fall into place and a composite picture is revealed. The statement released by the President of the United States crystalized any doubts. Simultaneously there was a subliminal click in the mind of the public. Things got very clear very quickly. Further, and unfortunately for law enforcement, once it was revealed evil incarnate was in the East St. Louis City Hall checking diamonds – $50 million in diamonds – there was an exodus from the Eads Bridge to the East St. Louis City Hall. You always go where the money is even if you cannot get a share.

CHAPTER 39

It is often said – and is quite possibly true – the *Carnevale di Venezia*, the Carnival of Venice, is the grandest masked celebration in the world. If there is any one thing the Venetians do well it is celebrating. The annual festival is more than a week in length and ends with Lent, 50 days before Easter. The name itself is the epitome of the celebration. The word comes from the Late Latin *carne vale*, and means both "farewell to meat" as well as "farewell to flesh."

For good Christians, the former definition is fitting. Lent begins on Ash Wednesday and ends about six weeks later with Easter Sunday. During this time period the devout will embark on a period of preparation for Easter by doing penance, repenting sins and self-denial of worldly pleasures. Once past Easter the true believers can return to whatever lifestyle they enjoyed before the next Lent. For the true believer, carnival, the "farewell to meat," means meat cannot be eaten during the six weeks of Lent.

For others – and particularly the Venetians – the term *carnival* has an earthier definition. The "farewell to flesh" is interpreted in the sense that one's inhibitions are released. Individuals can lose their everyday identities – and carnal restraints – behind masks. Fasting and abstinence are replaced with gluttony and anonymity. That, in a nutshell was an apt description of the crowd around the front of the East St. Louis City Hall and its two adjacent walls. It was a carnival in the American sense of the word. It was a fun place to be with no downside. After all it was far from the Eads Bridge. Yes, there was a police cordon around the building, but the men and women in blue seemed to be enjoying the scene. When the crowd began to chant things like "DROP ONE FOR ME" implying a diamond, the police joined the celebration by pointing to themselves just as the crowd was doing.

The fourth side of City Hall, the back, had nary a soul. There was no crowd here, just a dozen bored men and women in blue. There were some empty armored vehicles and about every half-hour a solitary patrolwoman was escorted through the line. She could enter the back of City Hall unescorted and her dozen men entourage settled into the crates and boxes on the landing dock and waited for her return. It was a typical assignment for them, hurry up and wait.

The crowd gathering at the Eads Bridge was a far cry from the carnival swirling around the East St. Louis City Hall. This was where the action was going to be. The bomb – what all the law enforcement people kept calling an "explosive device" – was going to be detonated here. Talk about a Fourth of July Extravaganza! It was going to make the fireworks over the Mississippi look like match sticks thrown into the sky. And the bridge! When it leaped for the heavens it was going to be something to see!

But there was a problem.

Actually, there was not a problem.

If the so-called "explosive device" in the Eads Bridge went off there was not going to be much left of either St. Louis on either side of the Mississippi. So, if the devastation was going to be extensive, "leaving the area for your own safety" did not make much sense. Besides, if the cops were staying, the danger could not be that great, eh?

So the crowd stayed.

And the mob blocked the entrance to the bridge on both sides of the Mississippi – roadway, passenger bypass and rail line.

Within an hour of the Lizzard press conference, the East St. Louis City Hall was surrounded by a mob of looky-loos. News cameras and reporters appeared out of the woodwork and everyone in the crowd had a chance to express their opinions because, with a 24-hour news cycle you had to fill 24 hours with something other than the outside wall of the East St. Louis City Hall. Hotdog, popcorn, pop and sandwich merchants serviced the crowd. The taverns and restaurants lining the streets around City Hall were ecstatic. Anyone could get beer or wine in a plastic cup from any one of a dozen establishments within a block or two from City Hall. The police were more concerned with crowd control than arresting bar patrons on the sidewalk with intoxicating liquors in plastic cups.

The crowd surrounding the East St. Louis City Hall had a carnival atmosphere. It was something different in a city where nothing exciting ever happened. Parents brought their children to the outskirts of the crowd and high school students on summer vacation thronged the approach to City Hall. It was a joyous gathering even after someone posted a YouTube of an explosion caused by Minor Uncle I, the predecessor to the bomb in the boxcar. The devastation was not alarming enough to sober the crowd. To the contrary, it invigorated them. Everyone in the mob expected the Eads Bridge to leap skyward at the end of the countdown. Cell phone cameras were primed for the event and everyone was taking bets as to when the bridge would leap to the heavens.

Everyone wanted to see what was going to happen next.

CHAPTER 40

F ifty million *dollars* in diamonds?" Jerry O'Reilly nodded his head in disbelief. "Some guy in City Hall is getting $50 million in diamonds?! Like they are just giving him diamonds like coffee beans in a bag?!"

"That's what the paper says. $50 million. That's what he wants. Looks like he's gonna get it too." Jerry's wife Lucile held up the special edition of the *East St. Louis Gazetteer*. "50 million smackers."

"I'd like to have just one of them smackers. Half of one anyway."

"Maybe we should see if we can get one."

"How'd we do that?"

"Well, there's an old utility tunnel under City Hall. My daddy put in telephone cables in the days before cell phones. He had to do a lot of crawling around down there. Chances are the tunnel or conduit or whatever it's called is still there. You might be able to crawl your way into City Hall. Bets are everyone is trying this keep this bad guy from getting out. There might be a chance for you to slip in. Nothing ventured nothing gained. Maybe you could get in, snoop around and maybe find a diamond or two what got dropped in a hallway."

O'Reilly looked at his wife. "You serious?"

"Sure. Why not? Finders keepers. If you found a $10 bill in City Hall it'd be yours, right? Diamonds are just like $10 bills. If you find it, you keep it."

"So you think I outa slip into City Hall and look for loose diamonds lying in some hallway?"

"Maybe you can help those diamonds get loose," she smiled. "Or you can sit here and let someone else come up with the same idea and watch him walk away with the glory."

O'Reilly thought for a moment and then said. "Where'd you think that telephone cable tunnel opened up outside City Hall?"

CHAPTER 41

There is an old aphorism in the construction business which asserts As-builts are actually "As-intended-built," "As-should-have-been-built," "As-were-intended-to-be-built" or "As-designed–before-budget-cut-built." In reality, "built" is up and thus blueprints become the "As-intended-built" and only after the fact are the blueprints adjusted. If at all.

This is particularly true the further east you travel. While it is possible to find people in Los Angeles who can remember when a high rise was a vacant lot, one would be lucky to find the great-grandchildren of the tenants who were evicted out of their high-rise to make way for a skyscraper in any East Coast city. Smaller buildings east of the Mississippi like the East St. Louis City Hall had a myriad of lives before they became what they were in the 21st Century. And, with each transubstantiation, blueprints, as-builts and as-intended-builts piled one on top of another with no one exactly sure what was actual and what danced through an engineer's mind in the days before rebar. In most cases, no one cared.

Such was the case of the telephone cable conduit which snaked through the netherworld of East St. Louis. In the early days of telecommunication, a "phone call" was a verbal transaction transformed from sound to numbers which were sent down the copper wire – both numerical sequence and copper wire being in the singular because only one message could be sent down the copper strand at a time. This meant a massive number of copper wire strands were required to serve the city's phones. Since these wires were underground, the conduits had to be large enough to allow those wires to octopus block to block and neighborhood to neighborhood as well as allow room for a tunnel technician to crawl through and replace defective copper wires. Fewer copper wires were required when technology made the leap from a single strand for a single phone call to line sharing. Then came fiber optic cables and strand by trunk line the copper infrastructure was abandoned. With the leap the cell phones, the only landlines in most buildings were for the dwindling number of in-the-wall telephones and FAX machines.

Since it was more expensive to extract the dinosaur-age copper wire in the conduits than could ever be recovered from copper sales, the copper wire in the conduits was either left in place or enough were extracted to allow for the installation of the fiber optic cable and the one-time pass of a technician through the conduit to shepherd the fiber optic cable to its new moorings.

It took O'Reilly a good six hours to find the conduit cover his father-in-law remembered he had been ordered to weld shut in 1956. Or 1957. The old man also remembered he and his crew had not actually welded the cover shut. They had left it loose because the hollow was a most excellent place to cache beer and Scotch – not to mention cool enough to keep their lunches from overheating when on the job.

The conduit cover had ended up as part of the drain system for a high-rent apartment high-rise which had slowly transformed to a low-rent high-rise and thereafter a slum dwelling. The old man was sure the conduit was still without welding because, frankly, why weld down a metal plate if you were only going to have to pry it open again if there was ever a flood in the basement.

It took O'Reilly three buildings to find the right tenement and two lies to get into the basement. Had the landlords looked at his Public Works badge they would have seen it had expired two decades previously and had the unmistakable visage of a Southern European with a name ending in "ini," not a man of Irish extraction with strawberry blond hair and freckles. His father-in-law had been correct; the conduit cover was still not welded. Even better, there was enough room in the tunnels below for a man to slither.

But not much more.

Slither O'Reilly did but it was not pleasant.

He was quite lucky because the journey from the tenement to City Hall was a straight shot. He did not appreciate this fact until he was into the conduit squeezing between the copper wire husks and the wall. As he crawled there were off-shooting tunnels, presumably to provide communication strands to other buildings in the immediate vicinity. Someone could get lost down here. Clearly to keep the tunnel creepers from getting lost, small metal plates had been affixed to the walls of the tunnels. But the script on the plates was in Hittite as far O'Reilly was concerned. He had brought his own Sharpie and made markings on the top of the conduit, an effort which turned out to be wasted.

Also of no value was the compass he was carrying. The North needlepoint jack-rabbited in every direction indicating a lot of magnetics in the conduit. The GPS on his phone was equally worthless. The flashlight was necessary because it was pitch black.

Belly-crawling most of the way with occasional hand-and-knees stretches, he scrapped the block and half to City Hall without much problem. At the end of his journey he found his entrance blocked by the double door of an electronic closet, the remnant of the days when "electronic" and "copper wire" were synonymous. He gave it a slight push and the twin doors opened just enough for him to see it was secured by padlock with a long shank.

A single padlock with a long shank in the days after 911?

What were the people in City Hall thinking?

He shinned his flashlight through the crack in the electronics cabinet but all he could see was the back of a door and boxes piled against metal shelving.

It didn't matter. He'd be back in an hour with his reciprocating saw. All that divided him from a stray diamond now was a shank of steel on a bicycle lock.

Chapter 42

The nine senior citizens had been at the Panhandler for two days now. Unfortunately, it had not been a pleasant retreat. Not with all the traffic noise and sirens blasting at all hours of the day and night. Something was happening, that was for sure.

"What's going on?" one of the elderly women asked Johnny, the clerk at the front desk.

"Oh, there's some kind of a robbery going on," he responded. "There's a bomb in the Eads bridge. It's closed off. That's all I really know."

"So we can't get to St. Louis?"

"You just can't use the Eads Bridge. Going to the game?"

The elderly woman pulled back her windbreaker to show a Denver Rockies top. "Absolutely. We are going to win big today!"

"Not so fast," snapped another elderly woman as she unzipped a jean jacket. She was wearing a Cardinals T-shirt. "Game hasn't even started yet!"

Johnny laughed and rang them out. "I'll take your luggage out." He smiled.

"I'll bring the bus around," one of the old men said.

Johnny counted the bags and smiled to himself when he saw one of the old ladies pawing through her purse. They had tipped well when they had checked in. He expected the same when they checked out. Old folks. Gotta love 'em.

CHAPTER 43

Justice, Defense and Homeland Security met, as usual, on Thursday afternoon. Today it was in the parking lot of the Smithsonian. They had no trouble assembling; they had been here before. No one had any documents to pass along so it was a casual, cordial discussion.

Defense told the other two all military personnel hardware had been withdrawn from within firing range of the Eads Bridge but were available on alert and on base. This pleased the other two because the withdrawal had been made public. "Good for a few votes," Justice said.

Homeland Security smiled. "The last thing we want is this George fellow taken down. He's got to slip away."

"He's got a perfect track record of that," said Justice.

"You are correct," replied Homeland Security. "All we have to do now is sit back and let him do what he does best."

CHAPTER 44

As George laboriously went through the stones one at a time, Noonan and Agent Hastings plotted their next move. All the communication between George and the outside world or, rather, the Command Center, was through by Rabinowitz. She would pick up black velvet bags of diamonds from what was called the "Diamond Desk" – though it was just a Formica table – and take the bags into George. George would go through the bags one at a time and await the next visit by Rabinowitz. Slowly a pile of black bags grew on one side of the table. On the other side were a collection of black bags, collections of stones George said were not adequate.

With one eye on the clock, Noonan took a trip down to the Command Center. He disliked being around so much politics but he had some questions about diamonds. He was loathed to be uninformed so he took a moment to educate himself. He had a half-dozen half-baked ideas as to how to stop George but none of them had risen to the level of serious consideration. So, as he was rolling possibilities over in his mind he took time off, to so speak, to learn more about diamonds. As he knew from experience, if you have a question, go to the experts.

So he did.

He went straight to the Diamond Desk.

He was not received well. First, he was not known by face or name to the three officers on the desk. Second, he was asking questions while they were feverishly working to keep up with George's demands.

"Hey, we're on a deadline here. And who the heck are you anyway?"

"Just the guy who's dealing with George. You have a few moments to answer to questions?"

"No."

Noonan gave one of those been-there-done-that smiles. "OK. I'll tell what I'll do. I'll get my commissioner on the Joint Homeland Security Commission to give me permission to ask you some questions."

The line worked magic.

It usually did.

"OK. OK. Be quick."

"I will." Noonan pointed to a pile of black bags on the far edge of the table. "What are those?"

"Those are bags with the stones George doesn't want."

"What's wrong with those stones?"

"They're cheap. I've got to say George really knows his stones. He spotted them as cheap right away. Took them out of the batches."

"What do you mean by *cheap*?"

"What do you know about diamonds?"

"Only what you are going to tell me."

The officer smiled. "In a nutshell, the larger the diamond the more it is worth. But it's also somewhat traceable courtesy of a software program called Gemprint. And since the 1990s, diamonds have been laser-marked. Now you can change the laser marks, but it is not an easy process. What George is looking for are smaller, high-quality diamonds. I'd show you a high-quality diamond but you would not be able to tell it from one of the cheap ones. They look alike to the unpracticed eye."

"What's the difference in value between a high-quality diamond and one of those?" Noonan said pointing at the pile of rejects in black bags on the edge of the table.

"Thousands and thousands of dollars. Some of the stones we have coming in are just a grade above costume jewelry. They look good if you don't know what you are looking at."

"Why are the jewelers sending in cheap stones instead of good ones? Are they trying to pull a fast one? Maybe give a cheap stone and tell the insurance company they sent in an expensive one."

The office laughed. "It doesn't work that way. First, the jewelers were asked for all their diamonds. We didn't know how many diamonds we would need so we just asked for all of them. Once they were prodded, the jewelers provided them. They just opened their diamond drawers and gave us the whole lot."

"Do they have diamond drawers?"

"Not the way you mean it. They have cabinets with diamonds in envelopes."

"How do they know which diamonds are worth thousands and which are worth pennies?"

"Each of the envelopes has a code linking it with a Certificate of Authenticity." He pulled an envelope off the top of a pile of envelopes. "See, this code?" He showed Noonan a string of letters and numbers. "This code is for the Certificate of Authenticity. Every stone is different."

"How different?"

"As different as fingerprints. That's how we tell stones apart. Think of the Certificate of Authenticity as a fingerprint on the computer. When we scan a stone, we get a fingerprint, if you will, of the stone. It's called a Gemprint. That's the program that fingerprints the gem. Once a jewel has a Gemprint, it's loaded into a database. Every one of these diamonds," he said as he spread his right arm out to indicate the diamonds, "has a Gemprint. Each diamond is unique and that uniqueness is a database. If a diamond is loose and in a jeweler's store, it's been Gemprinted. The only gems not checked are the ones going into jewelry. I mean, if a man comes in with his grandmother's diamonds and wants the jeweler to make a necklace pendant, the jeweler doesn't check the Gemprint of the diamonds. But if the man wants to sell the diamonds, yes, the Gemprint is checked. So is the laser-inscribed number. But, and this is a significant but, that laser-inscribed number can be changed. But it will take a r-e-a-l professional to the do the changing."

"So when the jeweler empties his drawer and hands over the Certificates of Authenticity, you are getting every stone he has. He isn't trying to pull a fast one."

"They would have to be very clever to get away with it. There is just too much paperwork. And every scrap of the paperwork would have had to be forged and in place when we showed up with the court order for diamonds."

Noonan picked up one of the black bags of rejects. It fit easily in the palm of his hand. "So, how much are these stones worth?"

"Without looking at them I could not tell. Let's just say a few thousand dollars."

"How 'bout those?" Noonan pointed to a similar black bag in the pile about to go to George.

"Depends. Maybe a hundred times more. Depends on the stones."

"Well, if the stones are fingerprinted like you said, isn't George going to have a hard time selling them?"

"Maybe. If the stones are sold in the United States. But these stones are primarily for jewelry. They end up in rings, pendants, tiara and other high end items. No one fingerprints those stones. No reason to."

"So George is going to sell the stones to people who will put them in jewelry?"

"Or sell them overseas. In East Asia no one is particular about where stones come from."

Noonan rolled a small black bag of cheap stones with his finger. "How much is this bag worth?"

"No way of knowing. You keep thinking every diamond has a specific value. It does not work like that. Every diamond is different and its price varies depending on where it is sold. It's not like a pound of bananas which will cost pretty much the same all over town."

Noonan emptied the diamonds onto the table and rolled them around with his index finger. He gave the empty bag a shake and asked if he could keep it. The man at the desk gave it a squeeze to make sure there were no diamonds inside and nodded in the affirmative.

"So how do you know when you have sent George $50 million?" Noonan asked.

"We won't know. We estimate how much we've sent him by how much the stones are worth here and now. In the right market someone could get twice its value here. Like I said, the value of diamonds is variable."

"I see." Noonan picked up a velvet bag with diamonds and rolled it around in his palm. "If this had nothing but good stones, the best diamonds. How much would it be worth? I mean, could I hold $50 million in diamonds in my hand?"

"Sure. If you had the right diamonds. But they would have to be very good to be worth that much. You can hold the Hope Diamond in your hand and it's worth about $200 million."

Noonan dropped the bag of diamonds on the table and pointed to some loose diamonds on the velvet spread. "Are these stones that good?"

"Some of them, yes. But the bulk of them are medium grade. Average to very good. There are a lot of top-notch stones, don't get me wrong, but $50 million? No. Not yet. Maybe $15 million now but not close to $50 million."

"So you won't reach $50 by the deadline."

"When's the deadline?"

"Six hours."

"Not a chance."

Noonan pointed to the bags of cheap stones. "What's going to happen to those stones?"

The officer shrugged his shoulders. "At the end of day I'm assuming they will end up with their Certificate of Authenticity and returned to the jewelry store they came from. Our instructions are to turn over whatever stones are left to the insurance companies. They are the ones footing the bill for the stones this George guy slips away with."

Noonan started to ask another question but the officer cut him off.

"Actually, let me revise that. The stones, all of them, good and bad," he swept his hand over the table, "were never *our* stones. That is, anyone's here. Technically and legally they are the insurance companies' stones. We just collect them, put them in bags and give them to an Illinois State Trooper." He struggled for a name. Noonan helped him.

"Rabinowitz."

"Right. Rabinowitz. She takes them to George. We don't own any of the stones. We just pass them along."

"How many insurance companies are we talking about?"

"Good question. I don't know. But you are asking the wrong question. See, there are lots of insurance companies involved in this, this, this,"

"Matter," cut in Noonan.

"Right, *matter.* There are lots of insurance companies involved. So, to make things easier because time was so tight, the companies agreed to let one large company bird dog the process."

"Bird dog?"

"You're not from around here, are you?"

"Not a chance. Nice country but too far from the ocean."

"To answer your question, the company overseeing the transfers is the East St. Louis Fiduciary. They are bird-dogging the, the, the,"

"Matter," Noonan finished. "Bird dogging. I like that."

"By the way, that officer Rabinowitz."

"Yes?"

"She single?"

"Why don't you ask her? Right now, you've got a lot in common."

"How's that?"

"You know what they say, 'Diamonds are a girl's best friend.'"

CHAPTER 45

Y ou want what?" Louis "Louie" Lone looked like a lobster. He had a ruddy complexion one associates with a lobster when it has been boiled. Which was why he was called "Louie the Lobster." He did not care. He was a desk man; not someone on the street. Property, actually. You didn't need a personality to work in Property, just be an obsessive bean counter. If there was a single term defining Louie the Lobster ,"obsessive bean counter" was it. He was the pen-and-ink man for East St. Louis Fiduciary. Thus, technically, those were his stones disappearing down the rabbit hole known as George.

Louie the Lobster was not happy when Heinz Noonan came calling. He was up to his elbows in piles of diamonds and certificates of authenticity and he did not have time for wild goose chases. He also did not have a sense of humor.

"You want what?" he snapped not sure he understood what Noonan wanted.

Just in case he was hard of hearing, Noonan asked him again.

Louie the Lobster shook his head even before Noonan finished speaking. He just stood there, shaking his head when Noonan asked a third time. When Louie the Lobster did not appear to be considering a response, Noonan gave one of those tired been-there-done-that smiles. "OK. I'll tell you what I'll do. I'll get my commissioner on the Joint Homeland Security Commission to talk to your commissioner who will talk to your boss's boss who will tell you to . . . "

This time the line did not work magic.

"You do that," snapped Louie the Lobster. "I don't have time for this kind of nonsense."

CHAPTER 46

After 911 it became a national priority to establish top-flight security for every public building in America. Public buildings were, after all, the most vulnerable targets for a terrorist attack. They could not move, hosted millions of members of the public every day and were a symbol of America's open society. *Crisis* creates *cash* and federal coffers opened to provide security for public buildings from Key West to the Arctic Ocean.

But East St. Louis, like many other cities in America, suffered from what is known as the "distance disease." The further away you were from Washington D. C., the less oversight there was on federal money. And, frankly, East St. Louis was as likely to be the target of a terrorist attack as the Lakers making the Super Bowl. So, after a flurry of widely-publicized security changes – including metal detectors at the front door of the East St. Louis City Hall and checking individual IDs – the rest of the Homeland Security money disappeared into the city budget through the time-honored process of fiscal osmosis.

Since no one was going to bomb the East St. Louis City Hall there was no reason to provide any security other than the front doors. The back and side doors already had security locks and the windows on all floors could not be levered open. The only need for security cameras was on the main floor and the alarms were only on the doors leading out into the real world. As far as the basement was concerned, "preparedness" simply meant putting coded locks on the doors.

On the outside.

No thought was given to the inside.

So, when O'Reilly cut through the shank of what turned out to be a bicycle lock (?!) and turned on the light in the basement, getting out of the room was as simple as turning the handle on the door.

Since the building no longer required copper wire telecommunication connections, the room had been transformed into storage. This was the junk room, for items which no longer had a value but were still not garbage. O'Reilly flicked on the overhead light and was pleased to see some of the items were old City Hall uniforms. They were all the same color so he assumed these uniforms were from people who had retired rather than gone through a changeover of style, color or cut. He found a pair of overalls and top that fit him and then scrounged around in the shelving for anything else he could use in City Hall. Luck was with when he found box of badges. The East St. Louis City Hall had no secrets so it had no electronic logins and thus, perforce, there was no need for electronic badges. If you wanted to go into a room, you just turned the door handle.

The only exception were the basement doors which had coded locks.

When O'Reilly opened the door to the basement and saw the coded lock on the outside, he knew exactly what to do. He closed the door and scrounged through the boxes on the shelves until he found a roll of duct tape. He ripped off a foot-long section and taped it over the latch bolt. When he tested the lock, the door was so old it slowly swung open. To keep the door closed but available for a quick exit, he put a small ball of duct tape in the door jam. It held the door closed. Now, dressed for success with a badge with a face looking vaguely like him, he carefully threaded his way up into City Hall.

CHAPTER 47

Rabinowitz, Noonan and Agent Hastings were having a Naugahyde night even though it was the middle of the day. There was nothing they could do but wait. All they could do was wait.

Cops are not good at waiting. They want to be up and around, doing something even if it is busywork. Rabinowitz was dealing with it in the worst possible way. When she wasn't delivering bags of diamond she was resting.

But, at the same time, this Naugahyde night was different – other than it was during the day. Though none of them said as much, they and everyone in City Hall were aware of the giant clock ticking away. To mix the metaphor, it was the gorilla in the room. But, in this case, everyone was talking about the gorilla rather than ignoring it. But then again, while time was getting shorter, no one had the ability to speed up any aspect of the matter. Diamonds came into the Command Center when they did. The Diamond Desk cleared then as fast as possible and every 15 or 20 minutes, Rabinowitz delivered the velvet bags to George. It was almost routine in terms of the task but, again, the clock was ticking.

For Rabinowitz, the waiting was particularly agonizing. Agent Hastings and Noonan had a century of experience combined. For them it was "been there done that." For Rabinowitz, it was the agony of "hurry up and wait." She was a line cop and her psyche screamed she had better things to do than sit on a couch and wait for the next delivery of diamonds she had to give to a perp.

Noonan looked over at Rabinowitz and said "You'd better get used to doing nothing. It's part of the job."

"Not this one. I should be out doing something. Anything. And here I am. Sitting. Sitting while some crook is getting millions of dollars in diamonds delivered to his room like room service."

"It is room service," said Agent Hastings slowly. "Right now sitting here is all we can do. There is nothing we can do. Actually, there is. Just hoping the troops can collect $50 million in diamonds before the clock runs out."

"That's not going to happen," snapped Rabinowitz. "There is no way the entire $50 million can be collected in the time we have left. We are not going to make the deadline. He's got, at the most, $20 million in diamonds."

"Rome wasn't built in a day," Agent Hastings said slowly. "I suggest you grab some shut eye. When things start to happen there is not going to be time to blink. Grab sleep while you can. When things pop you need to be awake and alert." With that he leaned back against the side of the sofa where he was sitting and closed his eyes. If he drifted off to sleep it was a fretful slumber.

"Can you believe that," said Rabinowitz somewhat quietly. "Sleeping at a time like this?"

"He's a pro," Noonan said. "He knows what he's doing."

"What about you?"

"I'm an old hand at Naugahyde nights. I may catch a few winks but I'm weighing possibilities."

"Like what?"

"We're missing a lot. I'll talk with you because you're new to this game. George and his team are professionals. They are meticulous planners. They have a time schedule and they are sticking to it. Everything they have done is in keeping with the time schedule."

"But many things can go wrong. Will go wrong."

"True. True." Noonan stretched. "At our end we have all the questions. We just must see how everything fits. George and his crew have been unpredictable. But they clearly want chaos. Why? The smart move – initially, I mean – would have been to use their knowledge of the railroad system to simply pull the boxcar with the bomb to a spot inside the bridge and abandon it. Then they could have called the two

Mayors and told them about the bomb and made the ransom demand. But they didn't."

"That's a *yes* for sure. They hijacked a train, kidnapped 70 people and stuffed them in an abandoned facility. What good was that?"

"A clever one. It was probably to keep the forces of law and order chasing on the wrong rabbit. Everything which the perps have done was for one purpose: to mislead us. Why the hostages? To waste a day and a half of our time looking for people. It got the troopers out of town while the police went after the diamonds. It cut our people power in half. "

"Why? What difference would it make? George was going to sit at a desk for 40 hours anyway. It seems like the hostages were just an added effort."

"I don't know. My best guess, it drew the press away for a day. Then, as you know, when the press got tired of interviewing the hostage families they got to interview the hostages. Then they got the bomb to concentrate on. Now the press is concentrating on the crowd outside around City Hall. I'm guessing it is a way to keep the attention of press focused."

"Oh, it's focused all right. This building is surrounded by press and the looky-loos and every nut with a cell phone camera. The Eads Bridge is locked down, all rail traffic is being shunted around the city, and if there were emergency on either side of the river the ambulance would need wings."

"All in the plan. How I do not know. But George does."

"And you think he's going to get away with it?"

"I don't know that."

"But you said earlier . . "

"What I and Agent Hastings said was it looks like the muck-ety-mucks were anticipating failure. So they are setting us up to take the hit. We are the expendables."

"You are so reassuring"

"No. But it does give us one very big advantage."

"If there is an advantage here, I cannot see it."

"Rabinowitz," Noonan started but Rabinowitz cut him off.

"If we're going to be on the sinking ship together, at least call me Rachel."

"Fine. Then call me Heinz."

"OK, Heinz. What's the advantage we have?"

"We know how cops think. So does George. What we have to do is stop thinking as cops and start thinking differently. We need to think outside of the box, off the wall. We need to be creative thinkers."

"How do we do that?"

"You do not defeat criminals like George by exploiting their weakness. You defeat them by undermining their strengths. George knows the weakness in his plan and he's got it protected. We have to undermine his strength. His strength is he is unconventional. Cops are not prepared for the unconventional and that's his strength."

"So we have to undermine his strength. How do we do that?"

"The quick answer is I don't know just yet. But we have to start guessing. We must try unconventional things. We should start preparing for what he *might* do. But what we have to do is *stop* thinking like cops. We have to think outside of the box."

"I'm not sure I understand."

"Let me give you an example. Suppose you are the principal of a high school. Over the Halloween weekend some of your students got ahold of a crane and dropped a pile of old automobile tires around the flag pole. You now have 20 feet of tires around the flag pole and the Homecoming Game is on Friday night. You don't have the time to rent a crane, it's too dangerous to use a chain saw, too slow to use acid, too hard to find the individuals responsible and have them remove the tires and too expensive to hire a helicopter. It's Monday afternoon. What are you going to do?"

"This sounds like a riddle. I hate riddles."

"No. This is real life. This is a real life example. This problem has been dropped into your lap. What are you going to do?

"I don't know. Off the top of my head I can't think of another way to get the tires off the flag pole."

"Exactly! See, you are thinking logically and rationally. You look at the problem logically and rationally."

"There isn't any other way to look at it."

"Not really. See, you are looking at the problem the way 95% of the people in America look at the problem. Logically and rationally this is a tire problem. Logically and rationally you try to figure out how to solve the problem as if it were a tire problem. But you can't solve this by assuming it is a tire problem."

"Well, excuse me, but *it is* a tire problem. The tires are around the flagpole. That's the problem."

"That may be the *problem* but the tires are not the *solution*. You are doing what 95% of the population does. You are trying to solve the problem by just looking at the tires. To be a creative thinker you must change your perspective. When a problem cannot be solved by thinking logically and rationally, you have to look at the problem from a different angle. You cannot manipulate the tires; you have to find something else to manipulate."

"Like what. I'm lost."

"You have tried and failed to solve this problem by coming up with a way to remove the tires. Now you have to manipulate something else."

"Like what? I'm still lost."

"Well, since you cannot get the tires from off the flagpole, why not see what you can do with the flag pole?"

"You mean bend it?"

"You could but it would be too hard and take too long. An easier way would be to get a forklift and raise the tires about three feet off the flagpole base. Then all you would have to do is unscrew the flag pole from the foundation. When the flagpole falls free you pull the tires off and then reattach the flag pole to the base."

"That's clever."

"No. It's off the wall thinking. All you have to do to solve the problem is change your perspective. You have to *stop* looking at the problem being one of the tires to one of a flagpole."

"What does this have to do with George and the diamonds?"

"Everyone is treating him the way you would logically and rationally deal with an extortionist. That's what he wants us to do. We have obliged him. Everyone is still obliging him. Everyone but you, me and Agent Hastings. We know he is going to do something off-the-wall, different. We are not counting on him to be predictable. Logically he is going to get the diamonds and then there will be a motorcade out to the bomb to shut it off. George is going to have to have some Plan B to get away after he has the diamonds and shuts off the bomb."

"How's he going to get away? We are going to be on him like white on rice every step of the way?"

"You are correct. George knows that. He must come up with a razzle-dazzle escape which works. It can't be a car because the bridge is packed. It can't be by rail because the line is shut down on both sides. He can hardly drop into the Mississippi because there are SEAL teams on the water and he can't fly away because no matter where he goes he'll be tracked."

"So how is he going to get away?"

"I don't know. But that's what we should be concentrating on. The key to resolving this case is figuring out how he is going to get away."

"Maybe he expects to get caught and then escape from jail."

"Good thought but he still has to get away with the $50 million. If he doesn't escape with the money the entire crime is a waste of time."

"Maybe the bomb is a fake and he intends to escape from here, City Hall. Maybe he has a helicopter pick him up and he just flies away."

"He'd still be tracked."

"Maybe there are old tunnels under City Hall."

"There probably are tunnels of some kind. Utility corridors and the like. But the minute he disappears you're going to have law enforcement in those conduits and watching every manhole cover within five miles. No, too complicated. His escape is going to be simple and ingenious."

"So what do we do? Just wait for him to get the $50 million and make a break for it?"

"We may have to. At this moment, I don't have a Plan B. "

"But you are working on one?"

"I'm always working on a Plan B. I don't know what he is going to do but at the very least I'm thinking about options."

"Options?"

"What ifs. What if he does use a tunnel under City Hall? Is there a tunnel under City Hall? Is there a zip line already installed from a window in City Hall where George and get away? Is there some kind of disguise hidden in City Hall George intends to put on, like, maybe a fireman's uniform? He hits a fire alarm and when the fire crews rush in, he walks out as if he were a member of the crew. Is there some kind of a glider hidden on the roof so he can slip away in darkness? There are a lot of what ifs."

"I'm sure all those escape routes are covered."

"I'm not. And I don't know that. You might want to double-check just to be sure. Why not come up with a list of the most outlandish escapes you can think of? Then junk the list. If you can think of it, other cops can too. George too. Then come up with something different."

"But it wouldn't hurt to double-check the obvious."

"It is never a bad idea to double-check the obvious. You never know . . ." He left his voice trail off.

"Well, I'll come up with a list. What are you going to do? Sleep?"

"Absolutely. It's going to be a long day when things start popping."

CHAPTER 48

What was it like being with all those people for a day and a half," Archie asked Whittaker, the **Bonanza** Engineer now out of a job, while they were standing beside a tank. It was a real tank. A United States Army tank. And it was not a relic. It was a bonafide, used in Afghanistan military surplus tank that had only been fired once. Then it had been shipped home. The Missouri National Guard got first dibs though no one knew what they would use it for.

Today they knew. It was half-on half-off the rail line running into the Eads Bridge, its turret facing backward, away from the Mississippi. Neither Archie nor Whittaker believed there was going to be an attempt on the boxcar but, then again, no one knew.

"One of the nicest things about being an engineer," Whittaker said, "is not dealing with passengers. Cargo doesn't talk back. But, no, it was not fun. Everyone blamed me for the hijacking. No one was happy."

"You must have been happy when the fire department showed up."

"ECCCstatic. Soaked to the skin because the fools set the whole place on fire. Grass, building, trees, everything. Then I got shuffled here."

"This isn't such a bad assignment. Nothing is going to happen. We're just back-up."

"To what? There's a bomb in a bridge that's going to blow in, what, about four or five hours. Why don't you tell me what we are doing here guarding an empty railroad line?"

"Orders, my man, orders. When you get to be my age you take them and smile." Archie gave a sardonic grin. "By the way, how did those terrorists get on your train? I thought everyone getting on any train, bus or plane had to be cleared."

"Getting on a train is not like getting on a plane. The passengers get screened if it's a commercial operation. But the FAM was a special hire. No one was screened; everyone was just matched to their ticket. How did the terrorist get on board? Who knows. Probably slipped on while the food and liquor was being brought onboard. Then they hid in the restaurant. We weren't out of St. Louis very long before they came out of hiding. It was an inside job, let me assure you. Whoever was in charge knew trains and how to disable the GPS and communication equipment."

"And uncouple the dome cars and hide them," Archie added.

"They were pros and they knew the nuts-and-bolts of rail travel. It will take a day or two but we will find the person."

"Yeah, but then these folks," Archie pointed down the tracks and made a flapping noise as he waggled his hand back and forth, "will be long gone."

"Probably part of the plan," Whittaker said sadly. "So far they have done everything right."

They were silent for a moment and then Whittaker looked at Archie. "I'm not a cop. I'm an engineer. How's this all going to play out? I mean, I don't see anyone letting the bridge get blown which means the bad guys are going to get the diamonds. But the bad guy is in the East St. Louis City Hall. The last I heard there were lots of cops around the City Hall building. I'm sure the guy has got have a plan of how he is going to get the diamonds, turn off the timer on the bomb and then escape. How's he going to do it?"

"That's above my pay grade. What will probably happen is he will get his diamonds and then give a stop code or a bomb override code. Something like that. Then he's in City Hall and the bomb is turned off. Then he'll have to make his escape from the City Hall building."

"But how's he going to escape? The building is surrounded."

"Oh, I'm sure he's got a plan. I'm sure it's a doozy too. No one is going to let him walk away with the diamonds if there is any chance the bomb is not turned off. And once the bomb is deactivated he's lost his edge. Why should we let him go if there is no threat of the bomb?"

"So he's got to have a way to deactivate the bomb and still keep the threat of reactivation until he gets away? That seems a bit much."

"You are right. But like I said. That's above my paygrade."

"So how's he going to do it?"

"Beats the heck out of me."

CHAPTER 49

Rabinowitz came back into the room with a strange look on her face. "He wants to see you," she said looking at Noonan.

"What a surprise," Noonan said as he rose from the faux leather couch. "I have been expecting this."

"Really?" Rabinowitz was shocked. "Is there something I should know?"

"Nope," replied Noonan. "All in George's plan. We've got, what, four hours to go and George does not have anywhere near the $50 million. He's got to reset the bomb. Logically he has to go to the bomb to reset it. We all knew this was going to happen. Now he needs me to be the go-between."

"Why you?"

"Rachel! Start thinking outside of the box! George has planned meticulously. He does not want the cops involved. Why? Because they have a command structure in place. Whatever he does the information will be instantaneously available to every uniform on both sides of the river. Me, I'm not in the command structure. By communicating through me he has put an extra layer of confusion into the mix. He didn't know I was going to be here but now he knows I'm here, he sees an added opportunity to throw sand into the well-oiled law-and-order machinery. Besides, he likes to gloat."

"So you'll talk to him?"

"Of course! It's all part of his game plan. Now, while I'm in there, see if you can find the list of events or gatherings we talked about earlier. There might be a clue as to what he intends to do on that list. We can't miss a single opportunity to throw sand into his well-oiled machinery."

CHAPTER 50

Realistically, O'Reilly never actually thought he would make it this far. He should never have been able to get into City Hall this easily. The buildings should have been locked down like a pressure cooker. But, then again, this was East St. Louis, a city where nothing ever happened. And that, in a nutshell, was why this George character was here. No one in East St. Louis ever expected him to be here and, as a result, the cops were absolutely, completely unprepared for the disaster that plopped onto their doorstep.

That was good news for O'Reilly. Here he was, in uniform, wandering the halls of City Hall with no checking his ID. Then again, there was no one in City Hall. First, because it was the weekend. Second, because it was a holiday. Third, because the police had the building surrounded to keep people out. Fourth, because no one expected anything to be happening inside City Hall but the delivery of diamonds.

It had not taken him long to assess the procedure. Looking out the back window of City Hall, the only part of City Hall where there was no crowd and police line, he had spotted a patrolwoman carrying little black bags into the building. He guessed these were the diamonds. Gambling she was going to be bringing the diamonds upstairs, he hid in the staircase on the second floor. If he heard her open the staircase door on the first floor, he'd slip across the hall into an empty room. If he heard the elevator start, he'd watch to see what floor the elevator stopped. The next time the patrolwoman came in, he watched the elevator indicator stop at the third floor. That was clearly where the diamonds were headed.

He hotfooted it up the staircase and sat on the landing with the exit door opened a crack. Twenty minutes later, the next time the patrol-woman came to the third floor, he saw her go to the end of the hallway and knock on a door. The knocking was in code, three taps and a pause, one tap and a pause, then three taps again.

So that was where the diamonds were going! This might be even easier than he imagined. He could be in and out of the room with a handful of diamonds in under five or six seconds, down the staircase to the basement in another 20 and into the conduit before the patrol-woman even knew there was a problem on Floor Three.

East St. Louis
Sunday, July 4th
High   92°
Low   71°
Precipitation: 0
Humidity: 54%
Wind: 7 mph

CHAPTER 51

It was time for East St. Louis Homeland Security Commissioner Mustafa Sanchez to start his 15 minutes of fame. Commissioner Lizzard had broken the ice which was acceptable because Commissioner Lizzard was going to be going home to wherever Sandersonville, North Carolina, was. But he, Sanchez, was going to be here in East St. Louis until the Resurrection. Long after he was gone, his grandchildren and great grandchildren would be talking about he had saved the day – AND East St. Louis AND the Eads Bridge – from certain destruction. At the very least it would show two ex-wives they had made a big mistake giving him the boot.

He loved this moment! Two days ago, he would have had to contact the press – print, TV, radio, tabloid, electronic and social media – and plead for their attendance at a news conference knowing full well only one in five so-called *news people* would attend. Not today. The *news people* were looking for him! Looking for an exclusive! They were responding to his twitter and RSS feeds. How the worm had turned! He knew the worm would turn again but by then he'd be in the history books.

He had read those history books. The greatest asset of anyone in any endeavor is surprise. You don't want your enemies to know what you were doing. That gave you the element of surprise. So Sanchez didn't tell the *press people* he was going to make an appearance. He didn't have to. They were in the East St. Louis Bond Hotel, the oldest and most exclusive hotel in East St. Louis and the reason Bond Street was so-named.

There was also another reason Sanchez was pleased this particular day. He was black and on July 1, 1917, a little more than a century early, there had been a massacre of blacks on the very spot where he was going to speak to the press. It was known as the East St. Louis Massacre and was one of the bloodiest race riots in American history. The rioting was so widespread the Illinois National Guard had to be called in to stop the violence. But by then an estimated 244 buildings had been burned to ground and, as blacks were escaping the burning buildings, whites had gunned them down. Many of the blacks who survived the flames had been lynched. Sanchez's father had been alive in 1917. His father had spent a lifetime as a janitor. Now Mustafa Sanchez, Homeland Security Commissioner for East St. Louis, a black man, was the man in charge of keeping East St. Louis safe. What changes a century had wrought!

Keeping with the element of surprise, Sanchez simply appeared.

He loved it when the press scrambled!

For him!

"Thank you for being here for this briefing," he began knowing full well there was no reason to thank *them*. (*They* should be thanking him for giving *them* something for the 24/7 news cycle was not more of man-and-woman-in-street interviews.)

"I do have a selection of items to report but I would like to ask your indulgence. Since many of you are new to this escapade I want to bring you up to speed as to where we are at this moment. For some of you this will be a refresher course and for that I apologize in advance."

The room was dead silent. This was his moment to shine! His father in heaven must be beaming in pride!

"Three days ago, as you know, three dome cars with travel writers disappeared off the rail line between here and Chicago. There was a full-fledged search for dome cars and passengers. The dome cars were discovered to have been separated and attached to other strings of box-cars and taken to three different destinations. The locomotive was left in plain sight and was discovered later. The hostages were discovered in an abandoned federal installation in upstate Illinois. This was the story dominating the news on Friday and Saturday."

Someone started to ask a question but Sanchez raised his hand, Moses-like, and the voice vaporized.

"On Friday afternoon, we did not know about the boxcar with the explosive device. The existence of the explosive device was revealed later Friday when a patrol officer of the Illinois State Troopers investigated a stranded Winnebago. The officer, whose name is being withheld at the moment for security purposes, was shown the explosive device in the boxcar. The officer was forced to copy the serial number of the explosive device, the VIN so to speak, and then told to deliver a message to the authorities. The terrorists – and they are terrorists – were demanding $50 million in diamonds to be delivered to a man named George who would appear in the East St. Louis City Hall."

He paused for emphasis.

"George arrived at City Hall and the building was immediately locked down. Because the explosive device is in the Eads Bridge over the Mississippi River, it is in neither Missouri nor Illinois, so a Joint Homeland Security Task Force was immediately formed. The Joint Task Force also includes North Carolina for the simple reason North Carolina has a terrorism expert on staff. The individual, and again, who will remain unnamed for security purposes, is working hand-in-glove with the Joint Homeland Security Task Force with the FBI. As we speak, all law enforcement agencies of both states are working to gather the diamonds demanded by the terrorists. The diamonds are insured. In dollar and cents terms, there will be no loss of revenue for either state or, for that matter, either of the cities of St. Louis. Our first concern is the safety and well-being of our citizens."

"It is now late in the afternoon of the second day. The terrorists initially gave us a 48-hour time limit and we are rapidly approaching the deadline. We do not anticipate we will be able to meet the terrorist's demand. As I speak, we are in the midst of negotiations to extend the timeline long enough to gather the stones he is demanding."

This, of course, was a bare-faced lie. The Joint Homeland Security Commission had never even said "boo" to George. There had been no negotiations. There were no negotiations. But then again. Sanchez knew it but the press didn't. The statement was not meant to be true or even hopeful. It was to cover the reputation of the Joint Homeland Security Commission just in case things went bad. They could always say *they* were acting in good faith but those terrorist, oh those terrorists. You just can't trust a terrorist!

"At this point in time we fighting analysis paralysis."

This was a term the three commissioners decided to coin to emphasize they were on top of the entire matter. It was a quotable tidbit and if they were in luck would be in the headline.

"Analysis paralysis is when you are paralyzed and take no action because you keep analyzing the situation. We do not have the luxury of time in this matter because events are moving incredibly quickly. Now, to be fair to the press, we will keep you informed of any progress. There will not be any regularly scheduled press conferences because events are moving too fast. But as details come to our attention, we will pass them along to you. At this time, all I can say is we are complying with the demands of the terrorist and we anticipate we will not meet his deadline. That is all I have to say at this moment."

"Let 'em stew," thought Sanchez with a smile plastered on his face. "It'll be the last them they put me on hold when I call."

CHAPTER 52

You want me to what?" snapped Louie the Lobster.

Lizzard and the other commissioners were in no mood to bargain or negotiate. "This is not a request," snapped Lizzard. "This is an order. You are to release all the diamonds in your possession. All of them. Without checking them for ownership, authenticity, nothing. We need to get this terrorist $50 million in diamonds *pronto*. Those diamonds," Lizzard said, pointing that the diamonds on Louie the Lobster's table.

"You can't tell me what to do," Louie the Lobster snapped back. Then he leaned forward and began a nose-to-nose conversation with Lizzard. "You are not my boss. You are not in my chain of command. No diamond is going to leave this table without being checked and logged into the system. If you don't like it, tell it to the Marines."

Sanchez tried a softer approach. "Louie, can call you Louie?"

Louie said nothing. He just stood behind the Diamond Desk and stewed – and lived up to his sobriquet.

Sanchez tried again. "Louie, this terrorist wants $50 million in diamonds. Just give him everything you have here," Sanchez said as he spread both of his heads over the table of diamonds and Certificates of Authenticity. "We already have the paperwork on every one of these stones. Just give the bugger his stones. We cannot afford to overshoot the deadline."

"Not a chance," Louis yelled more than spoke. "These diamonds, every one of them, are owned by someone and I am responsible for every one of these stones. One goes missing and I'm the one who takes the blame. You, you, you," he said as he pointed the index finger of his right hand at each of the Commissioners in sequence, "are nothing more than bureaucrats who got appointed because you didn't have the brains or talent to get a job honestly. You don't care about these diamonds. All you care about is dumping the blame for your own incompetence on someone else. Get your ruddy red behinds out of my sight. You want these diamonds, get a court order."

And that was how the conformation ended; Louie the Lobster, his face as red as a boiled lobster facing the three Homeland Security commissioners, their faces ashen white with rage, fear and frustration.

CHAPTER 53

"How's he been?" Noonan asked Rabinowitz as he prepared to see George. "You are the only one who's seen him consistently."

Rabinowitz shook her head. "He is one cool character; absolutely unflappable. I have to give him that. He has been the same every time I bring him diamonds. No fuss, all professional."

"No surprises."

"Just he's polite. I'm used to snippy perps, screamers of their rights. He's Tripe-C. Do you use the term in North Carolina?"

"Can't say we do. Triple-C?"

"Calm, cool and collected. One in 30 perps is Triple-C. They're the ones who are going to walk. They are the ones at the top of their game."

"George is Triple-C?"

"The poster boy for Triple-C."

"Well," said Noonan as he rose from the couch. "Duty calls."

"You know the code?"

"Been watching you do it for hours, yes."

Noonan went down the hallway and tapped the code on the door. He didn't wait for a response. He just tapped the code and turned the knob. The door was unlocked.

Inside the room was semi-dark. This was not because it was dark outside, rather, it was because George had the curtains drawn and all of the lights in the room were off save for a small, high intensity lamp on the table where George was working."

"Good of you to come by," George said as he looked up and allowed the loupe to drop from his right eye.

"You called and I am here."

"Captain Noonan! Have a sense of humor! This will all be over soon and as long as your side plays by the rules no one gets hurt."

"We are following your instructions to the letter."

"Not exactly," George smiled as he handed Noonan a small circular piece of metal. Noonan didn't have to examine it closely. He knew exactly what it was. "You don't seem surprised."

"I'm not," Noonan sighed and jiggled the metal object in his hand. "Standard FBI procedure. Plant a bug when you can where you can."

"Of course."

"You suspected it, of course. When was it planted?"

"Oh, a few hours ago. I knew it was coming so I graciously gave your charming Ms. Rabinowitz an opportunity to plant it in the brief case." He made a tssk, tssk, tssk sound. "I'm sure she was doing it on orders."

"Well, she is a clever lady. "

"Very. I'm impressed. I will be even more impressed if she did it on her own." George lowered his voice to a faux confidential tone. "Tell her I found the other one too."

"She planted two?"

"Clever lady. Probably figured I would find one and assume it was the only one. Good try. Tell her."

"I will. Was this the reason you asked to see me?"

"Not really." George swept his hands over the table. "Your people are working very slowly. I don't have anywhere near $50 million here. More likely half of that. You are not going to make the deadline."

Noonan was dead silent. He gave every impression of knowing this was going to happen. "I know that. You know that. I've known it for hours. So have you. Now, what's the next step?"

"That's an interesting question." George leaned back in his chair and locked his hands behind his neck. "I expected your people to move faster than they are. It should not have been hard to collect stones and have them brought here. I should have had all $50 million by now and be gone."

"That's neither here nor there, George. What we have here is a problem. You can either leave here with what you have or reset the explosive device and hope we can provide the balance of the diamonds in another 24 hours."

"True. But the first is out of the question. $25 million is about break-even for this matter. I do have expenses, you know."

"I am heartbroken," Noonan said with a chuckle. "So just go ahead and re-set the explosive device for another 24 hours. Then you can leave with what you have then."

"W-e-e-l-l," George drew out the word. "It's not so simple. See, I cannot reset the explosive device from here. I have to be in the bridge."

"In the bridge."

"In the bridge. I have to be on-site to do the reset."

"You expect us to allow you to go onto the bridge to reset the device? Why not just give us the combination to the lock and the code to the explosive device?"

George laughed. "You had to try that, Heinz. No, I'll do the re-setting."

"So we have to get you to the bridge?"

"Not unless you want to see the bridge go bye-bye."

Noonan thought for a long moment. Finally, he said, "Let me get this correct because I have to sell your idea up the administrative food chain. You have to be the one who resets the explosive device. Clearly we must figure a way to get you to the boxcar. You weren't planning on taking these diamonds," Noonan shook an open hand at the pile of black bags on the table, "with you?"

"You know that would never happen. If I took the diamonds with me," he tapped the pile of black bags, "what's to keep me from coming back?"

"You read me like a book." Again, Noonan thought for a long moment. "It is going to be very difficult to get you to the boxcar. Even if we could get you into an armored vehicle the streets are jammed with people. And that's just around City Hall. The drive to the bridge is not far but the approach to the bridge is clogged with people. It could take hours to get there."

"Not my problem, Heinz. You're a clever man. See if you can arrange it."

"Actually, it is your problem. I cannot go to Joint Homeland Security Commission with a problem. I have to come with a solution as well."

"With a solution?! That's their job!" He laughed. "But then again they are bureaucrats. They'd starve to death if they were locked in a grocery store. OK, if the streets are out you'd better think of an air exit. How about taking me in an armored vehicle away from the bridge, in the other direction? There's an airfield nearby. Then fly me onto the bridge in a fixed-wing."

"What's to keep you from having your gang snag you as we go to the airfield?"

"And leave all of this behind?" George pointed to the diamonds.

"George," Noonan said slowly. "No one trusts you. No matter what I propose the Joint Homeland Security Commission is going to be suspicious."

"Then watch your bridge go bye-bye."

Noonan stood for a moment and looked around the room. Finally, he said, "Well, the final decision is going to be made above my pay grade. But you do know there is going to be a lot of yelling and screaming."

George smiled. "My only regret is I cannot be a fly on the wall when you tell them you'll have to spirit me out of City Hall only to slip me back in an hour later."

CHAPTER 54

W hat did he want?" asked Rabinowitz. She stalled for a moment and then said, "OK. I know. Think ahead. I'll bet he is now playing us on the reset of the bomb."

"You're getting good at this," Agent Hastings said without a smile. "We knew this was coming."

"I have a few ideas," Noonan said as he gave a sad smile. "We have a little bit of time before I go to the Command Center. George is angling for the end game. What it is we do not know but there is something in the end game which cannot be changed, an event on that list is part of his escape plan. Do we have a list of local events that have been planned for some time?"

It had not taken Rabinowitz long to come up with a list of events and openings for the

Fourth of July weekend. It had been easy. She just punched up the East St. Louis Chamber of Commerce webpage and hit the "events" tab. The three of them looked over the list on the laptop screen.

"Well," Rabinowitz said when she saw what topped the list: the "Game of the Century" between the Rockies and the Thunders. "This one is off the list. The game starts in about an hour."

"I wouldn't count anything out," returned Noonan. "This guy is slippery as an oiled snake. He's sure to have a diversion. Something on this list is key to his escape, something whose timetable cannot be changed. What else is on the list?"

"Not much." Rabinowitz scrolled down the list with Noonan and Agent Hastings looking over her shoulders. "There are some local plays that start in the evening, a used book sale for the East St. Louis Library, some fashion shows, a gun show at the Sportsman's Arena, fireworks over the Mississippi River, a Fourth of July Saleathon at Jamison Brother's Volvo, and, what's this?"

The two men looked over her shoulder at the spot on the screen where she was pointing.

It was a jewelry exposition.

"Too obvious, I'm afraid," Noonan said shaking his head. "Something we would automatically assume was important."

"Well, it's the best we've got right now," said Agent Hastings.

Noonan agreed. "Nothing else seems to fit. You are right, however, we need to check it out."

"Well, I can't go," Rabinowitz tilted her head to the side indicating the direction of the Command Center across."

"I can't go either," Noonan said as he turned toward Agent Hastings. "I don't have a badge anyone will respect. Besides, I must take George's request to the commissioners. That kind of leaves you."

"I don't like this at all," Agent Hastings said showing emotion for the first time since he got off the Lear jet the previous day.

"I agree with you," Noonan said. "But you are the only one of us who can do it. On the bright side, if there is an angle, you'll spot it."

"Do you see an angle for George?" Rabinowitz asked hopefully.

"I don't NOT see an angle for George." Noonan tapped the list on the screen. "One of these events offers an advantage of some kind for George. Which one, I do not know. The most obvious is the jewelry show. How that's an advantage to George I do not know. But," Noonan smiled, "I'm betting George wants to misdirect us again. Unfortunately, it means we've got to check out the jewelry show. I'd hate to disappoint him."

CHAPTER 55

Over the entire course of his life O'Reilly had only come in contact with police routine once. It was when he had applied for a parade permit and had to develop an evacuation plan. To develop an evacuation plan he had been forced to deal with the police bureaucracy. It had not been an unpleasant task but it was tedious. It was then he learned the police department was just like every other organization in America.

Did he know the bureaucracy? He'd worked for the State of Illinois for 33 years! He'd worked in a dozen departments and for more than a handful of agencies. They were all the same. 90% of the people who worked there could care less about quality. They were hired to do a job and that was all they did: that job. Peeking at the police on duty in front of the East St. Louis City Hall he saw the same all-I'm-doing-is-my-job attitude. They were nothing more than crowd control. They held the crowd back. That was it.

He figured the patrolwoman delivering the diamonds had the same attitude. It was her job so she did it. She made two more deliveries to the third floor while O'Reilly sat on the staircase landing trying to come up with a plan that seemed feasible – and successful. He decided the best plan was to wait about ten minutes until after the patrolwoman had made a delivery. Then he would tap the code on the door. With luck, he could catch this George guy unprepared. He intended to snatch whatever diamonds he could off whatever table was there and beat feet for the basement.

But just as he had screwed up his larcenous nerve, there was a break in the continuum. This time the patrolwoman did not leave the Third

Floor. As O'Reilly watched she came out of the room where she had been delivering diamonds and walked three doors down. She didn't knock on this door. She just opened it and stuck her head in. She said something O'Reilly could not hear and two men came out. One was an old guy in his late 60s or early 70s. He was wearing Khaki pants and a blue work shirt, the kind you would see on prisoners. He was wearing boots which was odd because this was East St. Louis. People here – and specifically in places like City Hall – did not wear boots. Or khaki pants.

The other man was shorter but still about six feet tall. Whoever he was he must have spent a lot of time in Hawaii recently because he had an island tan broadcasting I HAVE JUST COME BACK FROM VACATION – ASK TO SEE MY PICTURES. He was dressed professionally, suit and tie, and had brown shoes. Definitely someone who knew how to dress for all occasions.

O'Reilly squeezed back against the back wall of the staircase just in case the three decided to come down the staircase. They did not. What they did do, however, was to stop just outside of the staircase door.

Talk about the Luck of the Irish!

The old guy, the one with the beard, was telling the man dressed well he would have to go to some kind of a jewelry show over on the north side of town. The younger guy wasn't so sure and there was a discussion. Not an argument; a discussion. The younger guy didn't want to go. The older guy said the younger guy was the only one who could go. Then the older guy said to the younger guy something about him being with the FBI. That meant the FBI guy had to go. The patrolwoman chimed in and the younger guy said he would go. He would not be happy about it but he would go.

Then came O'Reilly's break! The patrolwoman said she'd walk the younger guy out of the City Hall. She said she had to get another load of diamonds. Or another bag of diamonds. Something like that. She said she'd walk the younger guy out. The old guy said something like "see you soon" or "best of luck" and walked back down the hallway in the other direction. The elevator swallowed the patrolwoman and the younger guy and the old guy went into some office and closed the door.

Now all that was between O'Reilly and a handful of diamonds was a door at the end of the hallway – and he had the knocking code! All he had to do was wait about just long enough for the guy in the room to assume the knock was the next delivery.

CHAPTER 56

O'Reilly caught George completely by surprise. George unlocked the door when he heard the code and the next moment O'Reilly was inside like a bull in a China shop. George was no competition for a man who was half his age and 30 pounds heavier with every one of those pounds earned at a gymnasium. George was knocked aside like a leaf in a hurricane. Hurricane was a good analogy because that's what the inside of the room became. O'Reilly moved quickly, grabbed a handful of diamonds from off the velvet sheeting on the desk and he was gone. Out the door and gone.

Rabinowitz was on the second floor rising to the third on the elevator when she heard the pistol shot go off. Under normal circumstances there would have been a lot of background noise in City Hall so a gunshot would not have been heard beyond the floor where the explosion had occurred. But today City Hall was empty so the sound carried.

"What the . . " was all she could say and tried to urge the elevator to rise faster.

The last thing Noonan expected to hear was a pistol shot. Everything had been going smoothly. Now the pistol shot. Like a shot, in this case a physical spurt of energy, he was out of the vacant office on the third floor and into the hallway.

CHAPTER 57

George Orwell was famous for popularizing the concept of doublespeak. Doublespeak is the practice of disguising or reversing the meaning of the words being used. As an example, "downsizing" is a euphemism for firing people. "Productive" is what a diplomat says when the sides are in deadlock, a "political contribution" is a bribe, "collateral damage' means non-combatants are being killed and "enhanced interrogation" is torture. Historically there is the infamous Star Chamber, *Camera stellata*, which sat in judgment at the Palace of Westminster. The name of the court came from a star decorating the ceiling of the royal courtroom. Established in the last 15th Century, the original design of the court was to establish equitable enforcement of the laws when they were transgressed by socially and politically members of society.

This was a crock.

It was doublespeak.

There was no justice here; just politics.

The court may have been conceived as a bonafide legal entity but, as they say, the rich are different. So are the politically and socially connected. In essence, the court was established to free the politically and socially connected from having to appear with the unwashed masses. Convictions were only given when the transgression was particularly egregious. More sinister, to this day the term "star chamber" means a gathering of individuals of authority who meet in secret and pass sentence – in secret – against enemies of the members of the Star Chamber. There is no fairness involved as the verdict has already been decided and the court hearing is nothing more than window dressing to fool the public into believing the hearing was "fair and just." In the American West this was known as a Kangaroo Court because the court "jumps over" evidence in the defendant's favor and the judges are in someone's "pocket."

Over the years the name of the legal approach changed but the overall concept did not. In the 21st Century, "Star Chamber" and "Kangaroo Court" were archaic terms. But the underlying principle was not far from an archeological relic. The "power behind the throne" or, more appropriately, the "prime mover" was still there – it was just obscured by time, distance, vocabulary and bureaucracy.

As Noonan sat on the metal chair in the so-called "waiting room" to speak to the Joint Homeland Security Commission he was aware the three commissioners were simply the human face of the Star Chamber. The stench of politics was thick. These commissioners were not calling the shots; they were simply messengers. All answers were going to come from "on high" and these men were the lowest rung of the ladder – or ladders. So, making a short story even shorter, that was the way the game was played so here is where Noonan had to be.

But it did not mean he had to play the same game as the commissioners.

"We're being conned." Noonan had no problem being blunt when it came to reality. With more than a decade as a street cop in Trenton, in the days before he moved to North Carolina, he knew a con when he saw one. He didn't know how this con was going to play out but he saw George as more of a con than an extortionist. "He's been playing us for two days now. This is just part of his plan."

"How do you know that?" Commissioner Yang asked. And thus began the dance. A dance Noonan knew well. The street cop talking to the Assistant to the Assistant to the Assistant of the man/woman who really calling the shots.

Noonan continued as if he did not already know the outcome of the conversation. "Everything George has done has been misdirection. He operates out of a fog bank and pretends to offer us a peek of what's going on inside. But every time we get a peek and what when we get an inkling of what we *think* is happening, it turns out to be false. A red herring."

"You think this is red herring?" Commissioner Lizzard cut in. "This terrorist says he has to reset the explosive device. That's logical. What's wrong with the picture?"

"This is a highly sophisticated plot with a lot of moving parts. Yet, according to George, he has to reset the explosive device by hand? In an electronic age? No, he has something up his sleeve."

"You think this is part of his escape plan?" Sanchez was not going to be left out of the mix.

"I don't know," replied Noonan. "It's suspicious to be sure. Here we have a perpetrator, . . ."

Noonan was interrupted by the three commissioners, in unison, saying "terrorist."

"Terrorist, fine." Noonan stated. Then he restarted his sentence. "It's suspicious that just as the clock is starting to run out on a gathering of diamonds he suddenly realized it was going to take longer than 48 hours he suddenly feels a time pinch."

"But if we don't let him reset the bomb, er, explosive device, we could lose half of East St. Louis not to mention the Eads Bridge." This did not sit well with Sanchez. Yang nodded in agreement.

"It's your call, of course," said Noonan nodding toward the three. "But I think it's a bluff. If the bridge goes, so does he. I find it hard to believe he would put himself in harm's way."

"So you think we should not let him go?"

"It's an option."

Commissioner Lizzard cut in. "I'm not familiar with East St. Louis, but how far is this airfield from City Hall? If he wants us to take him to the airfield, are we taking an hour trip or a five minute one?"

"It doesn't matter," snapped Yang and then retraced his comment. "If what Captain, Captain. . ." he struggled to remember Noonan's name.

"Noonan," Noonan helped him.

"If what Captain Noonan says is true and this part of his escape plan – which I do not see because we are not going to let him go with any diamonds – then we have to expect some kind of rescue attempt on the way to the airport. The airport," he said looking sideways at Lizzard, "is not a regular airport. It is a landing strip for private aircraft."

"So it doesn't have any kind of security," Sanchez added.

"Well, if he escapes from the airport with no diamonds, what is the point of not letting him reset the explosive device?" Lizzard asked.

Noonan raised his hand chest-high. "We don't know how George plans to escape. But he does. Maybe he wants to get to the boxcar and affect an escape from there. Maybe he has a confederate in City Hall who will scoop up the diamonds while George is on the bridge. Maybe the diamonds are already gone, possibly dropped out the window to a confederate. Or they have been slid out the window on a zip line we don't know about. I have talked with him twice and the only diamonds I have seen were the ones which had just been delivered. The other diamonds are supposedly in little black bags. I've seen the black bags but that does not mean there are diamonds in those bags."

"That's a lot of possibles, Captain," Yang said. "We have to assume the men and women in blue have considered those options and shut them down – if they exist. As of this moment all we know for sure is an explosive device is set to go off in four or five hours. We cannot make the deadline this terrorist wants. I don't see we have any choice but to let him fly out to the bridge."

"But it doesn't mean we have to do it his way," interjected Sanchez. "He wants to go to an airport. If he goes to the airport he wants a fixed-wing aircraft. Landing on the bridge means we must clear away enough of the bridge for him to land and then take off again. That's what he wants. Fine. But let's add a twist. Suppose we pick him by helicopter from the top of City Hall. There will be no crowd problem at City Hall and no reason to clear off the bridge."

"That might be just what he wants," snapped Noonan and then backtracked a bit. "That is to say, George, . ."

"The terrorist," cut in Lizzard.

"Yes," replied Noonan hesitantly. "He is offering us a reasonable, unreasonable option. His offer to reset the explosive device is reasonable. Flying him to the bridge is reasonable. But using a fixed-wing aircraft is not reasonable. He figures we'll agree to the reset but not the fixed-wing aircraft. That's not reasonable. What is reasonable is the helicopter. He wants us to figure the solution he wants on our own. He wants the helicopter. Why, I do not know."

"So what do you suggest? We can't take a chance on the bomb, er, explosive device?" Sanchez was clearly nervous.

Noonan arched his eyebrows. "Follow his lead. He wants a fixed wing. Let's give him a fixed wing. He doesn't really want a fixed wing escort. He's trying to maneuver us into using a helicopter. Let's play his game against him. Agree to a fixed wing."

"But with no diamonds," cut in Lizzard.

"It makes no sense for us to let him leave with *any* diamonds," Noonan added. "But he is setting us up for something. What, I do not know. But it is all part of his plan."

Yang said something Noonan could not hear and then Sanchez asked Noonan to "wait outside." Noonan kind of nodded and then headed out into the "waiting room" which did not exist.

CHAPTER 58

It was an unusual meeting, not the usual, unusual meeting for Justice, Defense and Homeland Security.

And it was quick.

The consensus was clear. This George fellow had to "get away with it."

"We're being played." Defense was certain of that.

"Oh, that's a no brainer," replied Justice. "But why? The point of all the drama is the $50 million. If he goes to reset the bomb and does not take the diamonds he has, what's the point of an escape?"

"Who cares?" chimed in Homeland Security. "We have to keep our eye on the ball. What we want here is maximum publicity, minimum loss of diamonds, and no loss of life. If we are lucky and the gods are with us, this terrorist will escape, we keep the diamonds and the bridge stays up."

"This is all well and good but what do we do right now? The terrorist wants to reset the bomb. Fine, let him." Justice and Defense shook their heads in agreement.

"Oh, that's not the question," Justice cut in. "The real question is whether to let him have a fixed-wing or offer a helicopter."

"The terrorist asked for a plane. He's playing us. He really wants a helicopter," Defense added. "So let's give him a helicopter."

"OK," said Homeland Security. "But let's not make it too easy."

"*Au contraire*," cut in Justice. "Let's make it as easy as possible. If he leaves the diamonds and escapes, we come out smelling like roses. If he gets caught we're going to be fielding legal questions for the next decade. Let's keep this as clean as possible. Give him the chopper and see what happens."

CHAPTER 59

You are kidding?" Rabinowitz shook her head in disbelief. "they want to let George just fly out of here!?"

"That's what the commissioners ordered." Noonan was nonchalant.

"Something is very wrong here," Rabinowitz was stunned. "I do not trust George at all. Whatever he suggests there is a benefit to George. He had to know we could not collect the entire $50 million in stones, diamonds. So, what's his game?"

"Rachel," Noonan smiled sadly. "Don't spend your time trying to figure out the politics. Spend it trying to maneuver what IS happening into an advantage. We cannot change the political game. We have to do what we can with the ground game."

"But the point of the entire matter was getting the diamonds. If this is an escape, how's he going to get the diamonds?"

"I don't know. We are clearly missing something. We should be rolling possibilities over in our head. What could George be after if it's not diamonds. Maybe the diamonds are just a ruse. He's been misleading us around by the nose since the start of this matter. Is there something else in play?"

"Not that I can see."

"I agree with you. I don't see a solid Plan B here. But I also do not see George as someone who did not expect the timer on the bomb to runout."

"He is not a stupid man, I'll give him that." Rabinowitz looked toward the window as if there was an answer there.

"I agree," Noonan said. "He has a plan for everything. This has to be part of his plan. He's playing us like a fiddle. He suggested the airplane knowing we would reject the idea and substitute a chopper. He wanted the chopper in the first place. But why?"

"Oh, I'm sure it is part of his escape plan," Rabinowitz agreed. "But he's going to leave with no diamonds. How smart is that?"

"I see two possibilities," Noonan scratches his head. "Either the diamonds have no value to him and he's using them to misdirect us or there is something bigger he is eyeing."

Rabinowitz smiled. "I'll never be as smart as you, Heinz. I don't see him just leaving the diamonds on the table and disappearing into the ether. The entire point of the past two days has been $50 million in diamonds. And if not the diamonds, what's larger he could be after? Everything of value, like bank vaults, have been locked down for the past two days."

"How about the jewelry show?" Noonan replied.

"Agent Hastings is covering the possibility. He's doing it personally. "

"It's a possibility. I'm not so sure it's a possibility," Noonan scratched his beard.

"I agree. I think the jewelry show was just an excuse to split up the team."

"He's a clever man, Rachel. We have to expect anything from him."

"Well, if he's not after diamonds, what's left?"

"Rachel, that's what he wants us to think. He wants us spinning our wheels. We don't know what he has been doing in his room for all these hours. All we know, all I know for sure is there was a small pile of diamonds on the table when I went into the office. I really do not know if those other bags were full of diamonds."

"What's his angle?"

"Well, he could have swallowed some of the diamonds but even if he did he's not going to get out the door with $10 or $15 million in his stomach."

"I would not put anything past George," Rabinowitz snapped. "So far we've done everything his way. He's been conning us and this just another phase of his con."

"Oh, I agree with you 100%." Noonan shook his head. "But right now this is out of our hands. We cannot take the chance the bomb is a fake. George says the explosive device must be reset. We have no choice but to believe him. Rather, the Joint Homeland Security Commission does believe him."

"So George gets his chopper."

"Yup."

"But that's what George wants! We're being conned."

"I agree. But that's what the Commission wants. George will be allowed to leave City Hall in handcuffs and a waist chain. He will be escorted by a United States Marshal."

"And he has taken no diamonds."

"Correct."

"What if he has swallowed some diamonds?"

"I mentioned it as a possibility. George will have to, shall we say, evacuate himself at both ends to prove he has no diamonds in his system."

"That is *not* going to be pleasant for George."

Noonan just smiled.

CHAPTER 60

I guess I missed something," Lizzard said as he walked over to the window in the command center and stood next to Yang. The term "window" was a misnomer as it was actually the top of a second-story chute opening onto a slide. In its life before – and after – it was the Command Center, but the building was a warehouse and it was easier to slide boxes and crates to ground level rather than carry them down the staircase or use the elevator. The commissioners had established their office on the second floor, first because no one else was there and, second, because it gave them privacy.

Yang looked turned his head slightly sideways and raised his eyebrows. "Well, that's the way D.C. wants it done."

Lizzard was about to comment when Sanchez slipped up from behind. He took the other two commissioners by surprise.

"Don't do that!" snapped Yang. "I don't like surprises."

"Then you are in the wrong business," Sanchez laughed. "What the people on high want is a surprise for sure."

"No kidding," Lizzard said as he shrugged his shoulders. "They want him to have a chopper."

"That's the way the deal's to go down." Yang leaned over the chute and looked at the back of City Hall peeking out of the East St. Louis skyline ten blocks away. "He gets a chopper."

"But the diamonds stay," Lizzard added. "That's the only hold we have on him."

"Unless the diamonds are already gone," Sanchez added. "This guy is a surprise a minute."

"The terrorist," Yang quickly added.

"Yeah, him," Sanchez corrected himself.

"Well," Lizzard cut in. "We know the diamonds went into the terrorist. They did not come out in City Hall. We've had all kinds of law enforcement people scouring the outside of City Hall to make sure there isn't some surprise there. Nothing's been dropped out a window. There are no bags hanging out the window, any window. There is no zip line. No balloons have been launched and the buildings have been on lock-down for two days. He won't have any diamonds in his stomach or, or, elsewhere. He will have to be one bodacious magician to make $20 million in diamonds disappear."

"He's got some trick up his sleeve." Yang slowly shook his head. "I can't see his angle. He says he has to reset the explosive device. Fine. But he had to have known we could not gather $50 million in diamonds in 24 hours,"

"Maybe not," Lizzard added. "He might have thought with the power of two states and two cities we could have gathered the diamonds that fast."

"But we didn't." Sanchez added. "There is something wrong here and we just cannot put our finger on it. He has to effect some kind of escape with the diamonds. Without the diamonds an escape makes no sense. If he knew we could not collect the whole $50 million, he had some other plan in mind. With or without the diamonds he has to make an escape. So, fellas, what do you think? Is this reset part of his escape plan or a legitimate reset?"

"That's the $50-million-dollar question," Yang cut in. "But, look on the bright side, he's not going to leave City Hall with the diamonds whether he takes a plane or a chopper. He has to come back. So let him go."

"What if he skedaddles," Lizzard was looking at the angles. "What do we say then?"

"That's a low possibility," Yang shook his head. "I don't see that happening. He's going to be in a Trooper chopper. Even if he can get the trooper pilot out of the chopper and flies away, where's he going to land? He's going to be followed by aircraft and there are going to be patrol cars all over the landscape. He'll have to come down somewhere and then we'll nab him. What do we say if he skedaddles, to use your term, we catch him and say it was all it the plan. (pause) Our plan."

"But he won't go because he does not have the diamonds," Lizzard assured himself. "Why would he escape without the diamonds?"

Sanchez agreed. "As long as we are absolutely sure he does not get on the chopper with the diamonds, he can go."

"I still have a bad feeling," Lizzard said. "but I do not see him escaping with no diamonds."

"Even if he does," Yang finished the conversation. "We still look good. We stopped a terrorist attack, foiled a diamond robbery and can say we saved the bridge. Who cares where he goes?"

CHAPTER 61

It was Yang's moment to shine. Lizzard and Sanchez had their moment in the spotlight, now it was his turn. In his mind, Lizzard and Sanchez were pikers when it came to PR. Yang wanted to add drama to his presentation, something memorable. So, instead of holding a press conference in the Bond Hotel, he scheduled it for outdoors.

On top of a building.

Why?

Because he was from St. Louis. The *real* St. Louis. The big one, across the Mississippi River. Just because all the action was in East St. Louis did not mean he could not give his city a positive plug. He also wanted to press to know the *real* St. Louis was not East St. Louis – and East St. Louis had the highest crime rate in America. Not so the *real* St. Louis, his St. Louis.

Even more delicious, he was setting the time of his press conference to be just as the sun was setting. Then, from the top of the tallest building in East St. Louis, the press would be able to see the Gateway Arch in the distance, the most recognizable landmark in the Midwest. Why it was more recognizable than the Empire State Building which was, in actually, just a tall building among other tall buildings. But the Gateway Arch was unique. It was the tallest man-made monument in the Western Hemisphere, 630 feet of an inverted, weighted catenary arch reminding the world it was from here – or rather, there, across the river, where the wagon trains, mountain man and buffalo soldiers headed west. For those who dared the Great Plains, St. Louis, the *real* St. Louis, was the last piece of civilization until you got to San Francisco which, to be honest, until the Great Earthquake in 1906, was indisputably the wickedest city on earth.

Just to make sure the press conference was memorable, Yang planned the event strategically forcing the cameras to start on the Gateway Arch in the distance across the Mississippi River and finish with long shots of George getting into his helicopter escort from the top of the East St. Louis City Hall.

You could not get more drama than that.

CHAPTER 62

I t was an odd gathering. But then again, anything involving George was odd, unusual and unique. Noonan had never faced an adversary like George and he had a half century of experience with some of the most unusual perpetrators in America. But George was one for the books. Noonan and Rabinowitz knocked the code and were let in.

"Ready to go?" Rabinowitz was on guard. It was clear she did not know what to anticipate but expected anything.

"No," replied George. "This was not part of the master plan. I'm doing this for you," he said with bitterness." Then to Noonan specifically, "I don't want any games now, hear?"

"No games," Noonan replied. He pointed to the two men with him. "This is the United States Marshal Evan Swensen. "He will be escorting you . . ."

George cut him off. "You mean I going in chains."

Noonan shook his head sadly. "I'm afraid so." Noonan leaned toward him and stated in mock seriousness, "You know, a lot of people don't trust you."

George smiled. "I'll bet it is because of this." He stood up and swept his right hand over the pile of black velvet bags on the edge of the table and the briefcase.

"Well," said Noonan. "Some people are just naturally suspicious."

"Right," said George smiling. "You just can't trust some people. Let's get his show on the road."

"Well," said Noonan with a wry smile. "Before we go you have a duty to perform."

CHAPTER 63

O K," Rabinowitz was icy with professionalism. "Here is what is going to happen. You are going to be searched to make sure you do not have any weapons. You will be handcuffed and then secured to this man, United States Marshal Evan Swensen. You will then be taken up to the roof of this building where a helicopter will take you to the Eads Bridge. Once there you will be escorted down to the boxcar where you will be allowed to reset the code to the explosive device."

George cut her off. "Lighten up, Rabinowitz." He raised his hands and arms and allowed the Marshal to pat him down. "This search is least objectionable act I have done lately," he smiled.

As the Marshal was patting down George, Noonan moved around the table and stood next to George with the bulging brief case and pile of diamonds in black velvet bags directly in front of him. Noonan put casual hands on both the briefcase and pile of black velvet bags, leaned forward and said, "We don't want you taking any of these with you."

"Perish the thought," George said and gave a false smile. "I'll be back, you know. Then we can talk about my final exit." To the Marshal he said, "Are we through?" The United States Marshal mumbled something sounding like "yes," or "Uh huh." George shook his handcuffs. "Secure enough?"

"For your safety," Noonan said with mock seriousness. "The Marshal will put on the waist chain when we get on the roof."

"Well," said George as he limped sideways to get around the table. "Let's go. Time's a-wasting."

Noonan turned away from the table with George following behind him, limping past the table toward the Marshal, his hands in his pockets. Rabinowitz followed behind George.

"Don't you let anyone mess with my diamonds now!" George said with false bravado over his shoulder.

"I'm going to put a police seal on the door," Rabinowitz said in a flat tone. "Everything here will be just as you left it."

George laughed. "Thanks! I'll write you from Rio to say thanks."

Rabinowitz didn't say anything. George laughed. Noonan smiled as if to some inner joke while the marshal maintained the same external facial expression as Agent Hastings would have in the same, or any, situation.

CHAPTER 64

The reaction of the crowd around the East St. Louis City Hall was unexpected. One would have thought it would have been one of outrage. After all, everyone in the crowd knew that this George character was absconding with $50 million of their money. That was more than the total savings of everyone in that crowd. But that didn't happen. The reaction was the John Dillinger effect. The common man, the person in the street, was cheering the bad guy because he was robbing the rich. They couldn't rob the rich. They didn't have the means or intestinal fortitude to rob the rich. But here was someone who was bucking the system.

And clearly getting away with it.

The crowd surrounding City Hall did not know there were still diamonds on the table in City Hall. All they knew was that a helicopter had landed on top of the building and someone was being spirited away. Logically it could only be George and that somehow he had convinced, conned, connived the authorities to let him escape with the diamonds. He was getting away with it! Let's hear it for George!

Though the flight to the Eads Bridge was minutes in duration, by the time the chopper landed near where the isolated boxcar was located beneath the roadway, everyone on both shores of the Mississippi knew George was on the move. On both banks there was a mile of sunlight flashing on cell phone cameras raised to capture the arrival of this loveable scoundrel that was *getting away with it!* He was D. B. Cooper and Butch Cassidy rolled into one!

As soon as the chopper landed, a chant rose from one bank of the Mississippi and was picked up and passed along by press and cell phone internet coverage.

"GEORGE!"

"GEORGE!"

"GEORGE!"

CHAPTER 65

"We have lost contact with the chopper!"

The Illinois National Guard tracking monitor did not have to yell. All three commissioners were huddled around a tracking console on the first floor of the Command Center. The commissioners were not actively watching the console for two reasons. First, they did not know what they were looking at. That is to say, the console did not have a map of East St. Louis with a little blinking light showing progress. It had a screen with a blinking light on it, yes, but it took a professional to track the blinking light. The professional was a man in an Illinois National Guard uniform.

The second reason the commissioners were not hunkered down over the console was because there were three members of the press in the Command Center. The press – in the collective generic – had chosen three members at lot to represent all. So a newspaper journalist, television crew of two and a radio woman were present and recording the event, as Yang said, "for posterity." The media was writing, filming, recording when the man in the Illinois National Guard uniform issued the bad news in a perplexed, anxious voice.

The commissioners stalled in their interviews with the press and the press kept the pen, camera and recorder rolling.

This was the first moment the commissioners knew something had gone wrong. But how could that be? Every faucet had been tightened, every window locked, every escape angle covered, every contingency accounted for. George and a United States Marshal had boarded the chopper, George in handcuffs and the chained to the Marshal. The chopper had made it to the Eads Bridge and landed without incident. Another chopper had been an escort and there was a fixed-wing circling the vicinity. What could possibly have gone wrong?

"What the Sam Hill double-dog banana peel happened," snapped Yang. The other two commissioners looked at him in surprise.

"First time I ever heard that," said Sanchez with a smile.

"Gotta Christian woman for a wife," said Yang smiling. "And three daughters." He rolled his eyes. "The things I do for the church." When he saw the press watching he said, "That's not for publication."

"Well," Lizzard said with a smile, "the Sam Hill double-dog banana peel reality is that we've lost touch with the chopper. "

"How can you do that?" said Yang snapping back to professional.

"The chopper's still on radar but we can't raise the pilot."

"Well, what do we know for sure?" Yang was irritated.

The tracking monitor did not look up. He just spoke. "We know for sure the chopper with George, the pilot and a Marshal made it onto the Eads bridge. We have visual confirmation from blues on the bridge. They say there was some kind of a commotion near the boxcar and a single man ran to the chopper and got in. Then communications went ghost."

"But the chopper's in the air, right?" Sanchez sounded confused.

"Yeah," cut in Lizzard. "The military people here are tracking it," he pointed to the Illinois National Guardsman on the console." And there's a second chopper following it. But we cannot reach the pilot."

Yang, Sanchez and Lizzard looked at each other. Then, almost in unison they said:

"Why would the terrorist escape without any diamonds?"

"Has George escaped?"

"Where's he going?"

"Where can he go?"

"What the . . .?!"

"It can't be," snapped Lizzard. Someone is going to pay through the nose for this!" Then to the three members of the press he said, "None of this is for release. This is all a matter of national security."

CHAPTER 66

I f it were possible to call the confluence of human bodies a traffic jam, it was the perfect description of the front entrance to the Command Center. The three commissioners were moving toward the front double doors just as a representative from the United States Marshal Service powered through the same front doors and Noonan along with Rabinowitz came in from what could graciously be called the back door.

Everyone was coming for a different reason. The commissioners were on their way out to stop a runaway chopper, presumably full of George and a pilot who were flying with no communication equipment. The United States Marshal Service was coming to report the escort for George was handcuffed to the boxcar under the Eads Bridge – in his own handcuffs. Rabinowitz and Noonan were rushing into the command center with a long shot. There was absolute chaos for a moment worthy of the Keystone Cops, everyone being shocked by events they did not understand but were transpiring before their very eyes. It might have gone on for another handful of seconds had not a sudden shout come from across the command center floor.

"We've got movement," someone in the command center yelled.

Rabinowitz reached instantly. "What kind of movement?" she was yelling as she was running toward she believed the voice was located.

Noonan, the United States Marshal and the three commissioners scanned the interior of the Command Center trying to find the source of the voice. When Noonan saw Rabinowitz stop, he knew the source of the voice. "This way," he said casually and pointed to where Rabinowitz was standing looking at a screen. There was a mad rush to get to the source of the voice.

"What do you mean by movement?" Noonan heard Yang snap as he took up the rear. Looking over the shoulders of the troupe, Noonan saw the top of a head of someone with a set of earphones. He could tell it was a male by the voice. Noonan stood on tiptoes and could see the top of a blue-collar, most likely an Illinois State Trooper.

"What do you mean by movement," Yang said again.

The pate with the headphones did not turn. Clearly his eyes were glued to a computer screen or some electronic device demanding his complete attention.

"The helicopter has landed," the male voice said flatly. "I have it at the East St. Louis Centennial Stadium."

"That can't be," shouted Sanchez. "That's got to be some kind of an error!"

"Why?" Lizzard shouted.

"That's where the "Game of the Century" is being played! Between the Rockies and the Ravens! It's a stadium. The parking lot's full. The only place you could land that's not chock full of cars and busses is in the stadium!"

"He's going to land in the stadium?" Lizzard said incredulously.

"No, sir," came the response from the man with headphones. "The chopper is down in the parking lot. It has been in the parking lot for about 10 seconds. Patrol units are already en route. The movement I am tracking is a cell phone."

"Cell phone?" The question was so short and clipped Noonan could not determine who had said it. When the question was repeated, he realized it was Yang.

"What cell phone? Whose cell phone?"

"I don't know, sir. This unit was assigned to monitor and track the location of the homing device in the chopper. Then we were given a supplemental order by the United States Marshal's office to track the cell phone of the pilot of the chopper. When the chopper landed, the two devices began moving."

"Homing device?" It was Sanchez. "What homing device?"

"With all due respect, sir," came from a voice from beneath the headphones, "I am monitoring a real-time disaster. I cannot take the time to figure out *why* something is happening or explain the details of *what* is happening. I have been told the chopper landed and ground units are closing in on the parking lot of the stadium. My job is to monitor the location of the homing device and the cell phone."

"OK," snapped Sanchez. "Where's the movement?"

"I've got the homing device and the cell phone together. They are moving toward the stadium from the parking lot. I guess they are both in the possession of a single individual who is moving toward the stadium."

There was a buzz of questions as the gang of law enforcement individuals gathered around the tracking desk plumbed each other for details.

"Uh-oh!" ` It was the voice of the tracking console.

"I don't like the sound of that," someone said. Noonan did not recognize the voice. "What does 'Uh-oh' mean?" Someone asked and swore.

"The two devices have split up. I suggest this means we have two people on the ground. The cell phone location is hovering in the parking lot area. No, it is moving slowly to the southwest. Not very fast. About the speed of someone walking. The homing device is stationary. It is not moving at all."

"Keep tracking both of those devices," Yang said. "We'll send ground units. . ."

"They are already on their way, sir."

"But if they don't get there quickly we'll have lost George!" Lizzard almost shouted.

"I don't know anything about a George, sir. I just track devices."

"Don't stop!" Lizzard was on the edge of hysterics. "Keep tracking! Keep tracking!"

Noonan saw the pate of the man with the headphones turn back, clearly to look to see who was demanding he continued to do his job.

"Everything is under control, sir. The chopper landed and is being left the parking lot. As far as I know, there was only the pilot on the chopper. He . . ."

"Why can't we contact the chopper?" Sanchez was clearly confused.

"I was told, (pause) sir, (pause) the pilot is not responding. His communication system is most likely not operational."

"What does that mean?" Sanchez was irate.

"It means, (pause), sir, (pause) the pilot is not responding. There is no indication there is anything wrong with the equipment on board. Most likely the pilot does not have an operational microphone."

"You mean it is unplugged?" Sanchez was trying to wrap his head around the information flooding his way.

"Unlikely. If it had been unplugged and the perpetrator got out of the chopper the microphone would have been plugged back in. More likely the wire was cut. Like with a knife. Then when the perpetrator left the chopper the pilot had to fly to a secure location to get another microphone and head set."

"So we can't reach the pilot of the chopper?" It was Yang.

"Not until he gets a new headset, sir."

"That's pretty low tech," Sanchez snapped.

"Perhaps, sir, but very effective."

"Forget the chopper," someone pleaded. "We've got two people moving in opposite directions in the parking lot. The lot is going to be closed down in a matter of seconds. You keep monitoring the screen – or whatever device you have."

"Yes, sir."

"Where are the two people now?" Sanchez was suddenly all business.

"One is still moving slowing in a southwest direction. The individual is now out of the parking lot and continuing to move slowly."

"Make sure those coordinates are given to the ground units," Sanchez said on the edge of losing his temper.

"Already done, sir. Law enforcement units from both states and both cities are monitoring the same information I am giving you. They are moving faster, sir, because they are in direct contact with the units on the ground."

"Just keep doing your job, son," Noonan said from the back of the crowd. "Is there any indication as to the altitude of the cell phone?"

This time the pate with the headphones turned in his direction. "Sorry?"

"The altitude of the cell phone," Noonan repeated. "Logically the person with the cell phone would have to weave his way out of the parking lot around the cars. But you indicated the direction of travel of the cell phone was smooth."

"Well, I didn't say smooth. I couldn't say that. All I can say is the cell phone is moving in a certain direction."

"But you can't tell me if it's at ground level, can you?" Noonan was persistent.

"No. But what difference does it make?"

"We are dealing with a very clever, very well prepared perpetrator. He has been misdirecting us since the first hour of this matter. I'm assuming we are dealing with one person on the ground, George."

"But there are two devices in play," the operator was now looking at Noonan through a parting in the crowd. Now everyone was looking at Noonan with question marks in their eyes.

"Yes. That's what George wants us to think. There were only two people on the chopper. The chopper landed and one person got out. So we are tracking one person."

"But there are two devices in play. I'm tracking them! I must assume your person in the helicopter met someone on the ground. Two devices moving in different directions indicates two people on the ground."

"Maybe. You are tracking two devices but there is only one person on the ground."

"Not true," snapped Lizzard. "This George clearly met someone on the ground and gave him the cell phone. When we find the cell phone we'll have the person who's helping George."

"Probably not." Noonan scratched his beard. "That's what George wants us to think. He wants us to think there is someone on the ground. If we are convinced there is someone on the ground, we are going to spend valuable resources chasing a ghost."

"Well," said Yang with a snit in his voice, "if there isn't someone with the cell phone, how is it moving?"

Noonan smiled. "It's probably hanging from a balloon. A helium balloon. This reset of the explosive device was just a ruse. He planned on escaping during the reset. He suckered us. He knew we were going to settle for a helicopter. When all the details come out I'm sure we will find George had a weapon and a backpack of gear hidden in the boxcar. I'm betting he slipped the handcuffs off or maybe he had a key. Then . . ."

Sanchez cut him off. "How'd he get a key?"

Noonan didn't miss a beat. "He's been a step ahead of us the whole way. Police handcuffs can be bought anywhere. He might have put a key in his mouth. We didn't search his mouth. We weren't looking for keys. We were looking for weapons and diamonds. Then, when George and the Marshal walked over to the boxcar to reset the explosive device, he just opened the electronic lock and pulled out a weapon. An Uzi seems to be the weapon of choice. He probably pulled out an Uzi, unlocked himself, locked up the Marshal and commandeered the chopper."

Sanchez nodded in agreement, "And he left the Marshal's cell phone with the Marshal."

"Correct," Noonan said. "That's my guess. George wanted us to know he was on the chopper. So we followed the chopper."

"So there is no explosive device?" Lizzard was stunned.

"I don't think there ever was," said Noonan sadly. "When time runs out nothing will happen. One big dud."

"But the diamonds?" Lizzard was still staggering under the realization he'd been hoodwinked.

"Now it is clear the diamonds had nothing to do with this extortion."

"Terrorist act," snapped Yang.

"Fine," said Noonan. "*Terrorist act.* From the very beginning of this matter the overall assumption was this was a crime for profit. That's the way we looked at it. But it never was. Now we know. It was for the thrill of the crime, not the profit. The diamonds had nothing to do with it. We were played like a fiddle. George had this planned right down to the escape. We gave him exactly what he wanted."

"So he 'got away with it?!'" Sanchez was beside himself with rage.

"Not yet," said Noonan slowly. "Not yet."

CHAPTER 67

"What about the homing device?" Yang hovered over the man at the console like a melodrama Dracula over a sleeping Miss Universe.

"Stable, sir. There is no movement."

"This guy is standing out in front of Busch Stadium? What's he waiting for? If he goes in we'll never find him among the 50,000 people inside. Why's he standing outside?" Yang shook his head.

"I don't know, sir. All I can tell you is the homing device is stationary."

"How was the homing device planted?" Sanchez looked back through the packed bodies at Noonan.

Noonan smiled. "The FBI initially ordered two homing devices slipped in with the diamonds which were being given to George. He found them both."

"Well, one of 'em seems to be working," Lizzard said from the sidelines.

"True, true," said Noonan. "Actually both of them are working. One is still upstairs in the spare office. Officer Rabinowitz and I needed a Plan B. So, we re-planted one of the homing devices. George apparently did not find the hidden device. It is still on him. For the moment. He's a very clever man. He will find it. We just need to make sure we find him before he finds the homing device."

Yang's face was glowing red. "We will talk about this later. But why is he standing outside of the Stadium?"

Noonan was about to say something but Rabinowitz cut in. "George has been doing the exact opposite of what we expect for two days. My guess is he expects us to believe he went into Bush Stadium to look for him. It's the logical, rational law enforcement move. He hijacked a chopper and flew to the Stadium parking lot. He expects us to assume – again, the normal law and order way of thinking – is he is going into the stadium to get lost in the crowd. He expects us to flood the Stadium with law and enforcement personnel from two states, two cities, the United States Marshal's office and Homeland Security all armed with photos of George."

Noonan cut in. "But we have no photos of George and we do not even have a forensic drawing of him. Which means even if we do send our people into the stadium, they have no idea who they are looking for."

"But he won't be in the Stadium." Lizzard had a hard time wrapping his mind around the possibility. "That's not logical."

"Which is exactly why he probably isn't there. The only edge we have right now is he does not know the homing device has been planted on his person," Rabinowitz continued. "I don't know where he will be going. But if the homing device is stationary outside of the Stadium, he's probably waiting to be picked up. Then, while we are spinning our wheels inside the Stadium he's headed out of town."

"So we should *not be going* into the Stadium?" Sanchez clearly did not like this departure from the logical and rational.

"I did not say that, sir. What I might suggest is we set up a perimeter around the Stadium before anyone leaves. If he is in the Stadium we will probably never find him in the time we have. He looks like half of the people watching the game. But if he is standing there at the gate, he's waiting for a ride. There can't be many people leaving the game early. Not THIS game, anyway."

There was dead silence for a full five seconds.

"It's your call, Sanchez," said Yang.

Yang looked like a man who had just lost his lunch and dinner. He looked around the press of the crowd around the monitor.

"U-oh" came the voice of the console.

"That does not sound good," Noonan said as he leaned toward the console.

"He's gone ghost," said the operator. "The homing device is gone."

"He found it! What a bit of bad luck!" Lizzard stamped his foot.

"We'd better get cracking!" Sanchez had found his voice. Looking around he eyeballed Rabinowitz. "Do it! Do it! Coordinate with the United States Marshal. Go! Go!"

CHAPTER 68

"We are at the Stadium, no sign of a chopper." The voice came over a cell phone rather than a police radio. This was a terrorist act and as such there were protocols. The assumption always is the terrorist will be monitoring the police band.

"There won't be," snapped a voice on the cell phone. "Is there a place where a chopper could land?"

"Affirmative. It has police tape and emergency sawhorses."

"Nothing else?"

"Empty. Why are we talking on the cell phone?"

"We have to assume the terrorist are listening in to the police band."

"Affirmative, sir."

"Stay in place. There is a loose end."

"Affirmative, sir."

CHAPTER 69

Yes, sir," came the voice over a crackle on the police band. "We are at the location you ordered. We see nothing."

"Repeat."

"Nothing. We are in an empty field."

"There is no one there? No car? No truck?"

"Affirmative. Just other law enforcement and some Homeland Security wonks."

"Be polite! The whole world is listening. The terrorists are certainly listening as well."

"Yes, sir."

"Walk the field."

"Yes, sir."

CHAPTER 70

Sir, this is Sgt. Harrison."

"With the vacant lot search?"

"Correct, sir. We found a cell phone. It was attached to a balloon which had burst. What do you want me to do with the phone sir?"

"You are wearing gloves, Sgt.?"

"By the book, sir, by the book."

"Bring it to Property. If we're lucky we'll get a fingerprint or two."

"Yes, sir."

CHAPTER 71

The only saving grace was traffic was again moving across the Eads Bridge. Everyone in every car crossing bridge knew of the terrorist act and was eyeballing the empty boxcar as they approached the bridge. The denouement of the matter did not come a moment too soon. The "Game of the Century" had finished 45 minutes earlier and the bridge was bumper-to-bumper with 50,000 fans – some happy, others not so much – on their way out of town.

The men and women in uniform who had previously been safeguarding the boxcar were now on duty to keep the traffic flowing. It was an easy task because no one wanted to stop; everyone just wanted to look as they drove by. Why stop? There was nothing to see but an ancient boxcar with its sliding door wide open to reveal nothing inside.

As the traffic snaked across the Eads Bridge, no one in any uniform gave any notice to the rusting, ten-person mini-bus with the name of a generic Christian church in Kansas City painted below its windows. The logo of the church was a smiling family of four; mom and dad together with a little boy holding up a bucket of sand and a young girl tossing a beach ball in the air. The only thing unusual about the mini-van was it was packed with septuagenarians rather than families. But no one on the ground noticed and the mini-van left the bridge and disappeared in the western maw of America

CHAPTER 72

Homeland Security was standing on the steps of the Jefferson Memorial when her cell phone buzzed. She raised her hand and stopped the conversation. She listened for a moment and then said, "Secure all paperwork. This is a matter of national security. We do not want anything released to the public. Other than a press briefing stating all is well, refer any other questions to Homeland Security here in Washington." She did not wait for a response. She simply hung up.

"How lucky can we get!" Justice was ecstatic. "Our pigeon has flown. No one was injured, the bridge wasn't damaged and not a single diamond missing."

"We don't know that yet," cut in Defense. "There was an attempt inside City Hall to steal a handful of diamonds. We are not going to know if it was successful yet. The situation still has to be managed."

Homeland Security cut in. "There are no diamonds missing."

"But," started Justice and then realized what was being said. "You are correct, there are no diamonds missing."

"This could get tricky," Justice added. "We do not want to have any diamonds that were supposedly *not stolen* showing up on Gemprint. That would not be good news."

"That will be handled here in Washington by our people. The diamonds are the only loose end and our people are already on the it. All paperwork on the diamonds is not to be held until further notice. The insurance companies will compensate the jeweler for the loss and Homeland Security will make sure the insurance companies know there is to be no disclosure."

Defense was concerned. "But there is still Gemprint. Every one of the diamonds pulled from the jewelers had a Gemprint. That's an international database. We can't get into the database and eliminate the Gemprint. The Gemprint of the missing diamonds is already in the system."

"There are no missing diamonds," Homeland Security reiterated. "Once we settle with the insurance companies any misplaced diamonds," she accented the word *misplaced*, "will belong to Homeland Security. If they pop-up on Gemprint, to use your term," she said to Defense, "the matter is referred to Homeland Security. Then we'll figure out how to handle it – if and when it ever happens. Most likely they will be treated as inherited diamonds. Those gems were never fingerprinted."

"As long as it doesn't happen anytime soon," cut in Justice. "We do not need an October surprise."

"As long as we move fast there will be no October surprise. But we have to act quickly. We have instructed the Joint Homeland Security Commission to hold a press conference wrapping up the entire matter. In the press conference it will be mentioned the diamonds involved all had a Gemprint. That way if any diamonds are missing – and none of them are – the diamonds will be mothballed. We just don't need them to appear before the first Tuesday after the first Monday in November."

"Are the locals clever enough to add the tidbit into their press conference without raising eyebrows?" Defense was concerned.

"D. C. has already scripted it," replied Homeland Security. "They have been instructed to read the release word-for-word."

"This entire matter has to be finished quickly. We have to, I repeat, have to put this entire matter to bed today. Now." snapped Defense. "The President released a statement yesterday and will close the door on the matter today. We do not need anything else coming up – and particularly anything which contradicts what she is going to say."

"I agree," said Justice. "Fortunately we have a plug, a fail-safe." Justice looked at Homeland Security. It was an unspoken question asking for confirmation.

"Homeland Security has everything well under control," Homeland Security said smugly. "We have direct supervision of the three on-the-ground operatives. We expect no trouble. One is a detective out of a small town out of North Carolina and he will be back in his small town in 24 hours. His immediate superior is the Homeland Security Commissioner on the Joint Commission. We anticipate no problem there. The FBI agent on the ground was pulled from retirement which puts him out of the loop. Besides, he's FBI. Agents don't speak to anyone. Homeland Security has seized all the documents which will eliminate a paper trail for any journalist."

Defense smiled. "The last loose piece we have is the Illinois State Trooper, whatever her name is. She is going to be the problem. You know how women are."

"Hey!" snapped Homeland Security as she said, "We don't need that kind of talk here. We've got a woman in the White House."

There was a moment of silence. Finally, Defense added. "The item is neither here nor there. The State Trooper is a loose cannon. We need to move her off center stage. She's not going anywhere and will be in East St. Louis. She'll be a magnet for the press."

"Then let's get her out of there," Homeland Security said. "There is no place for her in Homeland Security and Defense is not a good fit. Can we find a place for her in Justice?"

Justice nodded. "Justice needs someone with street knowledge of East St. Louis. It's got the highest crime rate in the country. We can fund a position in the Governor's office for her. That will get her out of East St. Louis."

"We need her gone now," said Homeland Security. "Now, as in before the election."

"Done," said Justice. "She'll be on her way to Chicago by this time tomorrow."

"And she does not go back," Defense insisted.

"Not for four years," restored Justice. "We're up by 6% in Illinois, 3% in Missouri and two-to-one in the electoral account. She'll be in Chicago for at least four years. After that, no one is going to care about what happened inside the Eads Bridge."

If it were possible for bureaucrats to celebrate in public, the three would have been dancing in Lafayette Park with *sombreros* and chugging *Margaritas*. They were giddy with excitement. It was a win-win-win. The one with the widest smile was Homeland Security.

"Talk about a silver lining to a storm cloud! Why it's raining doubloons!"

Justice was equally ecstatic. "We have come out of the water dry! No diamonds gone. No bomb went boom. No one killed. Nothing but good press!"

"And the spin," Defense added. "We got the best of all headlines. The President, THE BLOODDDY PRESIDENT, has taken credit for halting a terrorist attack dead in its tracks, recovering an explosive device that was hijacked and scared – get me SCARED – the terrorist into fleeing ahead of schedule. You can't get better press than that!"

"Not a single diamond gone! Not one! Not one! This is total! Total!" Justice was giddy with excitement.

"Give those joint commissioners a raise! Get them on the circuit! We can squeeze a three percent jump in the polls. Three percent for standing down!" Homeland Security danced in the streets. "All we have to do is seize all paperwork. All of it. Homeland Security wants every bit, bite, memo and order in Washington D. C. under lock and key. Once into the Archives it'll sit for 75 years."

"Who gives a rat's patootie about 75 years," celebrated Justice. "We just need six months!"

CHAPTER 73

President of the United States

White House
1600 Pennsylvania Avenue NW
Washington, D.C. 20500

F OR IMMEDIATE RELEASE:
    July 4

"I want to thank the news media for allowing me this brief opportunity on Independence Day to inform the nation the crisis in the Eads
Bridge between St. Louis, Missouri and East St. Louis, Illinois has been
resolved. It has been determined the explosive device planted by the
terrorists has been deactivated by a contingent of demolition experts
from the United States Army Base in Fort Leonard Wood in Pulaski,
Missouri. I want to extend congratulations and thanks to our valiant
men and women in uniform who put their lives on the line to deactivate
an explosive device which could have caused extensive damage to our
nation's infrastructure – not to mention the possible death of hundreds
of lives of Americans. The explosive device is now harmless and the FBI
is actively searching for the terrorists who perpetrated this threat to our
national security.

It is important to thank the combined power of the Department of
Homeland Security and the Department of Justice for their rapid and
high quality response to this crisis. All personnel involved exhibited the
highest level of professionalism. Proof is not a single diamond of the

terrorist extortion was stolen. Quick and competent action by personnel in those departments were able to eliminate a terrorist attack and, at the same time, make certain the terrorist did not harm one life, earn the terrorist one dime or destroy one inch of American infrastructure.

Let me assure the American people the United States government and all its agencies and departments are actively and aggressively involved in the apprehension of the terrorists who perpetrated this outrage. They may be able to run but they cannot hide. We tracked Osama Bin Laden to his lair and we will not rest until these terrorists have been apprehended and brought to justice.

Once again I commend all personnel who were involved in this matter. All Americans owe these professionals a debt of gratitude. So, to all Americans, go out and enjoy what is left of the Independence Day holiday and if you see someone in uniform, thank them for their service to our country.

Thank you very much and God Bless the United States of America.

CHAPTER 74

It was not a happy group of campers who meet in the Star Chamber on the second floor of the Command Center. The three commissioners had arrived and arranged their respective chairs to be as intimidating as possible. Lizzard had suggested dark leather desk chairs and Sanchez had dipped into the emergency funds made available by Washington D. C. then, Sanchez wanted a "long counter' but the joint commission thought desks would be better – three of them – and Lizzard could take his back to North Carolina. All three got laptops as well.

All by special delivery because, well, you know, Lizzard had pointed out, there were only 48 hours to this matter and after that, who knew when they might get funding enough for "office supplies."

By the time Noonan, Agent Hastings and Rabinowitz were summoned – and summoned was the correct verb – the commissioners had already conferred for an hour. The stage had been set and the parts assigned. Lizzard took center stage – and sat center stage – because he would be leaving the limelight in a matter of hours. The other two commissioners would be able to bask in the glow of success for months.

Lizzard peered over his desk like an Inquisitor of the Spanish Inquisition at the condemned.

"Exactly what was going on up there on the third floor?" He pointed a boney finger at the three. Agent Hastings started to speak but Lizzard cut him off. "You are not in my chain of command. You will have to answer to your superior. And you," he pointed at Rabinowitz, "will make yourself available at the pleasure of the United States Marshal and the State of Illinois.

What we," he emphasized the word *we* as he swept his hands sideways to indicate the *we* in this case meant the commissioners. "What we want to know is just what happened up there on the third floor of City Hall. You have a lot to answer."

Noonan said "for."

"Eh?" Lizzard was taken by surprise.

"For. I have a lot to answer for. You left out the preposition."

Lizzard was puzzled for a moment. "OK, Captain. For. You have a lot to answer *for*."

"Where would you like to me start?"

This took Lizzard by surprise. "Well, at the beginning."

"Very well." Noonan gave Rabinowitz a wry smile. If Rabinowitz was shocked, surprised or amused she gave no indication. "I received a summons in Sandersonville two days ago when my commissioner of Homeland Security,. . ."

Lizzard cut him off. "Captain. We know all that. Let's start a little further along. What were the three of you," he indicated Rabinowitz and Agent Hasting," doing on the third floor?"

"Basically, Commissioner, we were supplying George, the extortionist.. . ."

"Terrorist."

"OK. We were providing George, the terrorist, with diamonds."

"Yes, yes, yes, we know that," Lizzard looked to his right and left. Noonan's easy going style was on the edge of insolence. "Captain, we need to know what happened on the third floor. I want to know what you and Agent Hastings were doing up there."

"And Officer Rabinowitz."

That infuriated Lizzard. "Of course, Officer Rabinowitz as well."

"Well, (pause) Commissioner, (pause) the bulk of the time toward the end when we were actually dealing with George, . . ."

"The terrorist."

"Yes, Commissioner, (pause) the terrorist, (pause) Agent Hastings was at the East St. Louis Jewelry Exposition. "

"What was he doing there? The terrorist was in City Hall."

"It was clear to us George," and Noonan quickly added "the terrorist" before Lizzard could correct him again. "had to be planning some kind of an escape. We came up with a list of possible exit strategies. The best one was something involving gems, *ergo* the jewelry show. Agent Hastings went to the jewelry exposition to see if there was any angle for George. He was at the jewelry exposition when the interloper appeared."

"Interloper?"

"The individual who appeared on the third floor and attacked George."

"The terrorist."

"Yes," Noonan corrected himself. "The terrorist. An individual appeared on the third floor and conned his way into the terrorist's room. He apparently grabbed a handful of diamonds and was making out of the room when George," Noonan caught himself and then added the word "terrorist" before continuing. "We, Officer Rabinowitz and I, did not know we had an interloper until we heard a shot."

"The terrorist shot the interloper?"

"No, Commissioner. There is no evidence he, the interloper, was shot. There was no blood anywhere in the room, the hallway or the staircase."

"I, we" Lizzard looked to his right and then his left. From the facial expression of the other commissioners it was clear this was the first time they had heard of the interloper.

"Come again," interrupted Yang. "I have never heard of any interloper."

"Things were happening very quickly, Commissioner." Noonan looked from Yang to Sanchez. "Things got very complicated very quickly."

"Before you go on, Captain," Sanchez said. "Let's finish with this interloper. He conned his way into the terrorist's room?"

"Correct," Noonan said. "Later Officer Rabinowitz discovered he had slithered his way into City Hall through a telephone cable conduit."

"A conduit? Was he a snake?" Sanchez spoke before he thought. Then he revised his questions. "What, exactly, is a telephone cable conduit?"

"In the days before cell phones, telephones were connected by actual wires. Copper wires. In those days you needed one wire for the entire phone call. So, to hook up all the phones in East St. Louis including the City Hall, a narrow tunnel had to be constructed under the city to house the wires. Underneath the city are all kinds of tunnels – I call them conduits – to handle the wires."

"But we have cell phones!" Yang interjected.

"Yes, Commissioner. But there were numerous in-between steps. As technology jumped forward, it was possible for one copper wire to handle more than one call. Then, as you said, came cell phones. There are still quite a few phones in City Hall hooked up on solid lines even though most people are using cell phones. Those telephone lines are still under the city. As the City of East St. Louis and the people of East St. Louis got more and more cell phones and fewer and few hardline phones were needed, the conduits under the city were abandoned. Somehow the interloper knew about the conduits. He entered the conduit a few blocks away and slithered into the basement of City Hall. He apparently came out in the basement and found some old uniforms and ID cards. He then went upstairs, hid in the staircase and watched Officer Rabinowitz tap a code on the terrorist's door. When Rabinowitz went downstairs, the interloper duplicated the tapping code and entered the terrorist's room. He grabbed a handful of diamonds and fled."

"And the terrorist shot him?" Yang said hopefully.

"Not as far as we know," Noonan replied. "As I said, there was no blood so we have to assume he was not hit."

"Did he get any diamonds?" Sanchez asked with terror painted on his face.

"We do not know," Noonan replied. "He knocked over the table in the terrorist's room when he made a grab for the diamonds. We found some diamonds in the hallway indicating . . ."

"You keep saying *we*," said Yang. "Who's *we*? I thought Agent Hastings was at that, that jewelry exposition."

"We, in this case," Noonan responded. "Was Office Rabinowitz and me."

"Where was Rabinowitz when this interloper entered the terrorist's room?"

"She was getting diamonds from the Command Center."

"Who gave him authority?" Sanchez asked. "I didn't."

"Her. Officer Rabinowitz," Noonan pointed to Rabinowitz. "The terrorist, actually. He stated he would only deal with her."

"Well, I, I," Sanchez did not know what to say. "Is she qualified?"

"I'm sure she is," Noonan looked sideways at Rabinowitz. "As you can see she is wearing the uniform of an Illinois State Trooper. She was qualified."

"Yes, Yes," said Sanchez awkwardly. "But shouldn't she have known there was an interloper in the building. Wasn't that her job?"

"Actually, no," Noonan cut in. Then he looked directly at Sanchez. "Security for the building was the responsibility of Homeland Security. We, that is, Agent Hastings, Officer Rabinowitz and myself have been specifically ordered to report directly to the joint commission on all matters. Officer Rabinowitz's role was specifically and only to act as a transportation link between the Command Center Diamond Desk and the terrorist."

There was silence for a moment and then Yang asked. "Did the interloper get any diamonds?"

"We do not know," replied Noonan. "We will not know until all of the diamonds have been inventoried."

"So we don't know if he got any diamonds?" Sanchez expressed concern.

"Correct. We do not know if he got any diamonds."

"And he escaped?"

"Officer Rabinowitz was able to find his point of entry. She followed the telephone cable conduit until she exited in the basement of a tenement about five blocks away. By then he was gone."

"So he could have some diamonds." Lizzard said nervously.

"He could have, yes, but he cannot do much with any diamonds he has. The moment he tries to sell any of the diamonds he's going to be caught. All of the diamonds are fingerprinted, Gemprinted."

"I see," said Yang. "What did the terrorist say about the interloper?"

"He just said, 'Everyone has to start small.'"

"That's it?" asked Sanchez."

"Yes, sir."

"OK. What happened next?" Lizzard struggled to seize control.

"The terrorist indicated we were going to run out of time with regard to the explosive device. He stated he would have to reset the timer. But the reset had to be done physically, by someone actually on site. He suggested he be flown to the Eads Bridge in a plane and he would reset the device."

"We are aware of that, Captain. We," Sanchez looked at the other commissioners. "We were unaware of the interloper. We know everything else up to the moment the terrorist got on the chopper. We know the explosive device was a fake and there was an Uzi and – apparently – the makings of a small helium balloon in the boxcar. We knew he took the chopper pilot hostage, cut the headphone wires with a knife and stole the pilot's cell phone. What we don't know is how you were able to get the homing device on the terrorist."

"It was a team effort, sir."

"I thought Agent Hastings was at the jewelry exposition."

"He was. The team at City Hall was Officer Rabinowitz and me."

"Yes, of course," said Sanchez. "But tell us about the homing device."

"Officer Rabinowitz had been ordered by the FBI to slip two homing devices into the diamonds she was bringing to the terrorist. She did and the terrorist found both of them."

"Did that upset him?" Yang was concerned.

"Not at all. He said he expected it."

"He expected it?" Lizzard was perplexed.

"Yes, Commissioner. The terrorist was well informed and well prepared. He expected the homing devices."

"So how did you replant them?" Yang was now interested.

"We were only able to replant one. Rabinowitz and I were not willing to believe the terrorist was going to come back for the diamonds after he left to reset the timer on the explosive device. To be safe we devised a backup plan. We guessed he might only want to take the best diamonds. If he was not going to come back, we figured he was not going to wait to get the entire $50 million. He was really going to settle for five or six million dollars. You can hold five or six million dollars' worth of diamonds in your hand. *IF* you have the best diamonds. We gambled when he left he would palm the best diamonds in one of those black velvet bags. We took a chance and got a bag of cheap diamonds and put the homing device inside. Then, when we were in the terrorist's room, officer

Rabinowitz distracted the terrorist long enough for me to place the bag of cheap diamonds on top of the pile of high quality diamonds on the table in front of George. Then, as I turned to leave, Officer Rabinowitz made certain to be behind the United States Marshal giving the terrorist just enough time to palm the diamonds in the black bag."

"So he took the bag of cheap diamonds and the homing device instead of the high-priced diamond." Lizzard chuckled.

"That's right, Commissioner. We traced him until he got to the Stadium. Then, as you know we lost him."

"He must have found the device," Yang said. "That is not good news!"

"When he did," Noonan surmised. "He disabled the homing device and disappeared. Poof!"

There was silence for a moment. Then Sanchez broke the ice. "Just one more thing, Captain," Sanchez said. "Where did you get the low value diamonds? Every diamond the terrorist received was checked and double-checked."

"When we first met the terrorist he gave us a bag of low-value gems. Agent Hastings checked them out with a jeweler. We left them in our room in City Hall just in case we might need them."

"You know that's a violation of protocol," interjected Yang.

"No," replied Noonan. "The cheap diamonds were still in the control of Agent Hastings. When we returned the diamonds to the terrorist we were returning diamonds to the person who originally requested them."

"No sticky fingers?" Yang was not being humorous.

"Of course not." Noonan said innocently. "Even if any of us had sticky fingers, to use your term, it would do us no good. All of the stones are fingerprinted. Gemprinted. It's a national identity securing software program. The minute we tried to sell the stones we'd get caught."

There was silence for a moment and then Sanchez asked. "The bottom line here is our terrorist got away with chump change in diamonds instead of millions. We gave it our best."

Then there was a long moment of silence. It grew so long Noonan looked at Agent Hastings and Rabinowitz. Both were stone-cold professional.

Finally, Lizzard broke the silence. "Captain, Agent Hastings and Officer Rabinowitz, this entire matter has been a matter of national security. Everything involving this matter is top secret. None of you, individually or together, can say anything about this matter to anyone. Ever. We are expecting the President of the United States to make a statement and it would be, shall we say, hazardous to your careers if any aspect of this matter is discussed out of this room. Discussion of any aspect of this matter is a felony. The only people authorized to discuss any aspect is Homeland Security. Is this clear?"

Noonan, Agent Hastings and Officer Rabinowitz nodded.

"Consider this a top-secret matter and, I repeat, you are to have no contact with any member of the press or law enforcement regarding what happened here. Is that clear?"

Noonan, Agent Hastings and Office Rabinowitz nodded again.

"Absolutely, positively, nothing. Not a word about the any missing diamonds, the interloper or the terrorist. Your lips are sealed forever." Lizzard was emphatic. "You are not to have anything to do with this case again f-o-r-e-v-e-r. Is that clear?"

The three nodded their heads.

"You are dismissed," Lizzard said imperiously with a wave of his hand.

Noonan, Agent Hastings and Rabinowitz turned to go when the door to the Star Chamber exploded inward and a man with headphones charged into the room. "That homing device has been turned on! And it's headed in this direction!"

CHAPTER 75

For the second time in less than 12 hours there was a human traffic jam at the bottom of the staircase from the Star Chamber. Noonan stood at the top of the staircase with Rabinowitz and Agent Hastings and watched the collisions.

"They do not have the slightest idea what they are doing." Agent Hastings said it in a flat, FBI voice. "Not a clue."

"You got that right," said Rabinowitz. "Not a clue."

"These are your people," Agent Hastings said to Rabinowitz pointing to the mass of humanity boiling at the foot of stairs. "Ever thought of moving on?"

"Just every day."

"Ever considered the FBI?"

"You write me a letter of recommendation, yeah. I need some juice."

"You're got it. And," Agent Hastings suddenly became avuncular. "The way you were treated in there is disgusting. I would not want anyone's daughter treated that way."

"Well," said Rabinowitz, "You write me a letter and I will do your daughters proud."

"I'm sure you will." Agent Hastings smiled for the first time since he had come to East St. Louis.

"For what good it will do," Noonan said as he extended his hand toward Rabinowitz. "I'll write you a letter too. But I don't think a letter from Sandersonville will do you much good."

"It's one more letter I didn't have this morning. Frankly," she looked at the two men, "whatever does happen it has been an honor working with you two. I've learned more than I can ever state."

"Aw, shucks," said Noonan mouthing a Western movie character. "It was nothin'."

The three of them laughed.

Then they heard a shout.

Looking down the staircase they saw the entire mass of heads looking up at them.

"What are you three doing up there," snapped Lizzard. "You're needed here."

"I don't know what you're talking about," said Noonan. "We don't know beans about anything that's happening here!"

CHAPTER 76

You don't know what a Gemprint is?"

Jerry O'Reilly looked at his brother-in-law with question marks in his eyes. "Not a clue. What's Gemprint?"

"Gemprint is a software program that fingerprints gems. I'm not going to ask where you got these two diamonds but if they fell off a truck there's a good chance they have been fingerprinted."

"So that means I can't sell them?"

"Bingo. Before anyone buys these diamonds," his brother-in-law juggled the two diamonds in his hands, "they are going to check the Gemprint database. If they were stolen," he looked at the ceiling when he said the world *stolen,* "the jeweler will have to call the authorities."

"So, if these diamonds were stolen," and O'Reilly looked at the ceiling when he said the word *stolen,* "they are worthless."

"Not really." His brother-in-law shook his head. "They are only worthless if you try to sell them. If you put them in a ring or on a locket the jeweler isn't going to check their Gemprint. All you have to do is say they were heirlooms. Think of diamonds like a car. You only check the ownership of a car when it's going to be sold. Mechanics do not check who owns a car when they are asked to repair it."

"But sooner or later the diamonds will be sold. Then they will pop up on Gemprint."

"Jerry, Jerry, Jerry! You are thinking like a businessman! Diamonds are not like bananas or automobiles. Bananas and cars have a market value. Diamonds do not. Only jewelers buy and sell diamonds. The rest of us keep them. The Law of Supply and Demand does not operate when it comes to diamonds. See, if some guy gives his wife a diamond pendant she is going to keep it forever. She is not going to sell it. When she is not wearing it she will keep the pendant in a lockbox. When she dies, her daughter will get the pendant and the daughter will keep it forever. When the daughter dies, her daughter will get it. It's called an heirloom. People do not sell heirlooms, even when times are bad. They keep them."

"So if these diamonds were in a ring or a pendant it is unlikely anyone will even check their Gemprint?"

"Correct. No jeweler is going to Gemprint a stone until it's up for sale."

CHAPTER 77

"What the Sam Hill Double Dog banana peel is going on?" Yang said to the operator at the console. There was a general look of surprise at his words.

"He's a Christian with a daughter," Sanchez said as explanation. "Makes his life easier at home."

There was a twitter of laughter.

"Well, what is going on?" Sanchez leaned over the console.

The operator of the console was hunched over a screen that was indecipherable to the gathering.

"Your homing device, the one the FBI planted, is moving."

"You mean the one that was turned off?" Sanchez wanted to make sure everyone was reading from the same sheet of music, so to speak. "There is a homing device, an FBI homing device, somewhere in City Hall. You are not talking about it, are you?"

"I am aware of the homing device that was in City Hall. That's been picked up by the FBI and turned off. This is the homing device that was outside of Busch Stadium. The one that was turned off. Well, now it's back on. I'm tracing it."

Everyone hovered over the computer console where a light could be seen flashing.

"Why isn't that on some kind of a map of East St. Louis," asked Lizzard as he pointed at the screen – or what passed for a screen.

The operator of the console did not respond to the inquiry. He was hunched over the console and simply said. "We've been on this for a few minutes now. When the homing device came on, we contacted you."

The operator looked up. "You are with the Joint Homeland Security Commission, yes?"

Yang bristled. "We ARE the Joint Homeland Security Commission."

"Fine, sir. Then I don't have to say this four or five times. That's what happens when I send messages to the police or United States Marshal."

"Who do you work for?" snapped Lizzard.

"I'm a Colonel in the Illinois National Guard," he snapped back. Then he looked at Lizzard. "My instructions are to be courteous, competent and informative. Now I have a job to do. Since you are here I won't have to send runners with up-to-date reports."

"No one meant any offense," Sanchez cut it with a smile. "It has been a harrowing two days and everyone, that is, all of us on the Commission, are jumpy. So, with apologies, what you can tell us in real-time?"

The operator turned back to the console. "Apology accepted. A few minutes ago, the FBI homing device came back to life at the airport. Apparently, the person who had the device knows how to use it. It was turned off. Now it is turned on. Maybe it was bumped and turned back on. I don't know. I am not up-to-speed on FBI hardware. All I can tell you is that the device came back to life at the airport."

"But you said it was coming this way," said Yang.

"Yes. The device came back online near the airport. Then it started moving."

"On a plane?" Lizzard asked.

"No. It's on the ground in some vehicle. We are tracking it and it is snaking through the city."

"Snaking? Is that a specialized term for your profession?" Sanchez asked.

"No. When I say snaking I mean it is not moving directly in any direction. It moves from spot to spot, stopping occasionally for a minute or two and then moving on. There is no pattern. That is, the movement is not predictable. It is not something we can track in the sense it is stationary. I did inform the FB and I presume they are working with law enforcement. But there is not much anyone can do until the device is stationary long enough to identify the vehicle hosting the device."

"Those homing devices are pretty sophisticated," snapped Sanchez. "What do you mean you can't track it precisely?"

This time the operator didn't even bother to look up. His voice was tinted with the same-old-same-old technical explanation made simple for non-techies. "GPS is accurate to within ten feet as long as the homing device is stationary. Even then, if it is in a car, for instance, there are more than a few cars within ten feet of the target car. Even if you knew you were within ten feet of the homing device in a car, there could be five or six cars within the ten-foot range. Then, when the cars split up, you have to know which car to follow. Until the homing device is stationary long enough for us to get a fix on it and there are no other vehicles within ten or fifteen feet, all we can do is track it."

"But you said it was coming this way," said Lizzard with nervousness in his voice.

"That's correct. It started at the airport on the edge of town. That is, if you don't live here you'd think it was on the edge of town. Now it's snaking its way this direction."

"What's at the airport. Rather, what's near the airport?" Lizzard asked.

"No homes if that's what you mean. Just the airport," Sanchez said. "There's a private landing strip out there, the main sorting facility for the United States Post Office, a FedEx and UPS facility, a lot of support facilities for cargo handling, food preparation for in-flight meals, aircraft mechanical repair and stuff like that."

"Who cares what's there?" Yang was nervous. "We should be concentrating on finding the homing device."

"That might not be a problem." The man at the console looked up. "I've got the device located in our parking lot."

"Here?" Yang and Sanchez looked up in surprise. "At the Command Center?"

"Yup. Right here. It's on the move. It's coming inside."

In unison, the crowd around the console turned and looked toward the entrance to the Command Center. Then, in a single motion, those with handguns drew them. Like hornets from a nest which just been struck by a baseball bat, they scattered. With drawn guns, they concentrated their aim at the double doors of the Command Center. Everyone else in Command Center, sensing danger, scattered like leaves in a whirlwind. The Command Center was dead quiet for a full five seconds.

The twin doors which opened onto the parking lot slowly swung inward.

Two dozen handguns were aimed at the doors.

Into the Command Center walked a UPS delivery man who stalled in his tracks when he felt the crosshairs.

"UPS," he said as he raised his hand and let the package he was holding drop to the cement floor. "Don't shoot!"

CHAPTER 78

The bride was stunning. It was not a conventional wedding by any stretch of the terms: conventional or wedding. The bride's father was Irish Catholic and her mother was a Heinz 57 from Hoboken. The groom's father was Italian Jewish, his mother a Quaker from Montana. His brother was gay and her sister was a recovering Episcopalian. There was everyone you needed for a family reunion: a drunk uncle, a wayward hippie from the West Coast, a blueblood octogenarian wondering how he had spawned such a crowd and a matron who just wanted the event over, the newly-weds on the road and the kitchen cleaned up before midnight.

Juliette nee O'Reilly and now Cohen buried her face in her father's shoulder pads. "I am so happy, Daddy. I am so happy."

Jerry O'Reilly nestled her against his jacket and kissed her on the top of her head.

Juliette pulled back and put her hands behind her ear lobes displaying the twin diamond studs. "I am so, so honored you thought to give me a family heirloom."

"I'm glad you like them dear. They have been in the family for a long time. You deserve them."

"Oh, Daddy! I will keep them forever. I'll give them to my daughter, your granddaughter when she gets married. We'll keep them in the family forever!"

"A very good idea, darling. A very good idea."

CHAPTER 79

E dward Paul Lizzard III, Boris Yang and Mustafa Sanchez were as giddy as children on their first trip to the zoo. Everything which could possibly have gone right had. Every hostage in the dome car episode was alive and well. All dome cars were recovered undamaged. The locomotive had been undamaged as well. The explosive device in the Eads Bridge had not so much as scratched a hand railing, the terrorist was in the wind and every diamond – almost – had been saved. They had nothing but good news for the press.

"Echoing the words of the President of the United States," Boris Yang began because he was the last to speak to the press the last time, "we have excellent news for the residents of East St. Louis – both of them." This "both of them" was designed to be humorous and the press responded appropriately. "In a nutshell, it is a great day for America. We have stopped what could have been a monstrous terrorist attack from occurring, saved every dime of the ransom money, scared the terrorist into fleeing the scene of his crime and restoring law and order to the streets of America in general and the both cities of St. Louis in particular."

There was a general cooing of congratulations and the sound of many held breaths being expelled. The press had known the matter was over but the details had yet to be released. The words of Yang were as welcome as an "all clear" horn at the site of a disaster.

"I will not go into the details of the failed plot to kidnap 70 of our residents for $10 million or the terrorist act to extort $50 million in diamonds from our twin cities. Those details will be provided courtesy of my two distinguished colleagues, men who stood with me, shoulder-to-shoulder, as a team in facing down this terrorist. Together, as a team, we have shown what cool heads, a clever plan and the determination to do what is best for the people of the twin cities – and the United States of America – can do when faced with the raw power of terrorism. Americans can sleep soundly tonight because we have proven the distinguished men and women of the Office of Homeland Security are on the job, diligent and prepared for any terrorist who dares to step onto American soil. Our victory here is a small one, but it should be an indication to every terrorist anywhere in the world we, the citizens of the United States and the Office of Homeland Security, are ready for them any time anywhere."

CHAPTER 80

Agent Hastings was like the Lone Ranger: short on accepting thanks and long gone by the time the dust settled. But then again, that's how FBI agents are. They do their job and they go away. In the case of Agent Hastings, Molokai was calling. His job in East St. Louis was finished and he, like George, was in the wind.

"I didn't even get a chance to say 'good-bye,'" Rabinowitz said shaking her head as she leaned against the edge of the desk in the vacant room on the third floor of the East St. Louis City Hall. "One moment he was here and the next he was gone."

"That's the way people of sweat are, Rachel. They do their job and move on. They don't need medals or handshakes of congratulations. They just want to move to the next project."

"But he's retired!"

"You can do a lot in retirement. Life does not end when you hang up your badge."

"Are you ever going to retire?"

"People of sweat never retire. They stop being cops or accountants or lawyers and use their skills as counselors for nonprofits organizations, political organizers or church volunteers. You'll see someday."

"I'm not worried about someday. I'm worried about tomorrow."

"Oh, you'll be OK. Trust me. You are going to be transferred up the administrative food chain. Right now you are a hero and no one harasses a hero. Then you'll be moved up and out. It's called a lateral transfer. Your people do not want you on the street talking about what *really* happened. They want you long gone. The best way to have you long gone is move you out of East St. Louis into a job that has something to do with terrorism. Probably in the capital somewhere."

"You believe that?"

"Read your history, Rachel. Do you know who Laocoön was?

"Not a clue."

"You do remember the story of the Trojan horse?"

"Everyone does."

"Well, let me take you back to the morning the Trojans looked over the parapets of their fortress and saw the Trojan horse. The plains were empty of Greeks but there was a giant horse. The Trojans streamed out of Troy and stood around the horse marveling at it. Everyone was asking what it was and why it was there. Almost everyone thought it was gift."

"Almost everyone?"

"Except for a priest by the name of Laocoön. He took one look at the Trojan horse and said, 'I don't trust the Greeks even when they come bearing gifts.' His warning should have been the first clue something was wrong.

"Then Laocoön grabbed a spear and threw it against the side of the Trojan horse. When the speak struck the horse it made a hollow sound indicating the statute was empty and, depending on the ancient source; a moan came from inside the horse. That should have been Clues Two and Three there was something wrong with the horse."

Rabinowitz thought about it. "Considering what happened, why didn't the Trojans listen to him?"

"Because Laocoön upset the gods something fierce. They caused a giant earthquake to shake the ground and ordered giant serpents to rise from the sea and devour Laocoön and his sons. Next time you are in front of a computer, pull up Laocoön on Wikipedia. The statue of Laocoön and his sons being devoured is one of the most famous sculptures of the Roman Empire."

Rabinowitz cut in. "I know the rest of the story. The Trojan horse goes into the city, a small group of men came out from inside and they open the gates to the city. Why are you telling me about Laocoön?

"Because Laocoön has been the symbol of what happens to the people who tell the truth no one wants to hear. He was devoured by giant serpents. Today we do not kill people for telling the truth. We either retire them in such a way they are not going to upset anyone's apple cart . . ."

"Like give them lots of retirement money as long as they keep their mouth shut?"

"You put it some tactfully," Noonan said smiling at Rabinowitz. "But yes, if they are old. If they are young like you, they bump them up to good jobs making good money. Then it is made clear you can keep the good job making good money as long as you continue to have selective amnesia."

"*Amnesia* as in forgetting George sent back all the diamonds he had palmed when you slipped . . ."

"When *we* slipped," Noonan corrected her. "You were a principal in that bit of prestidigitation. I placed the bag where I was sure he would palm it. You maneuvered yourself and the United States Marshal perfectly so George could unobtrusively pick up the bag and put it in his pocket. You did a masterful job. We were a team, Rachel, don't ever forget that."

"I thought it pleasant when George sent the diamonds back to me by UPS. That was a surprise."

Noonan chuckled. "When Agent Hastings opened his UPS package and found the FBI homing device he did not look happy."

"He shouldn't have been. George got in one last jab. He got away with it again! Do you think George is ever going to come back?

"I doubt it. I think he and a handful of his like-minded elderly retired friends decided to pull off a scam. They were probably bored to tears and wanted one last bit of excitement. They weren't after the money. It was never about the money. They craved the excitement. You will learn in life you do things for money or satisfaction. When you are no longer happy with the money or satisfaction, it's time to change your lifestyle."

"So George is not coming back."

"These people came away clean. No one was hurt. No money was stolen. Everyone wins."

"Do you think George would have returned the diamonds if they had been the real valuable ones?"

"Oh, I think so. Like I said, it was never about the money. It was all about the thrill of the matter. He knew every one of those diamonds had a Gemprint. He could not sell them. So he returned them. He didn't want them."

"With enough time we'll figure out who they were."

"Nope. My bet, no one is going to be looking for anyone. There is no crime here. No one has been injured, the bridge is intact and no diamonds have been stolen. It is an out-and-out win for Homeland Security. Those three commissioners are going to get a Niagara Falls of terrorist-fighting money. They are not going to want anything to upset their applecart."

"So nothing is going to happen?"

"Nada. Zip. Goose egg. Take your impending promotion with a smile and occasionally, send me a postcard."

"Send one to Agent Hastings?"

"Naw. He's doing just fine on any beach in Molokai. No need to remind him again of the 'one that got away.'"

CHAPTER 81

Louie the Lobster was unimpressed by Lizzard, Yang or Sanchez, individually or collectively. Diamonds may be a girl's best friend but they were also his responsibility. Every one of them. Every single diamond of any value collected by any law enforcement officer and delivered to the Diamond Desk of the Command Center. Those diamonds were his babies. Rather, they were the responsibility of East St. Louis Fiduciary.

Every one of them.

He had to account for every one of them.

Every one of them.

So, when he was told there was a possibility not all of the diamonds – his babies – might show up after the terrorist matter was completed, he thought the worst of the best of the men and women in blue. They had sticky fingers and this baloney by Homeland Security was nothing more than a cover-up. Who did these yokels think he was.

So they didn't tell him.

They told his boss's boss's boss.

In New York City.

Who called his boss's boss.

Who called his boss.

Who told Louie the Lobster he was retired.

With a fine pension – along with a nondisclosure agreement.

If he signed within 48 hours.

CHAPTER 82

H einz Noonan, the "Bearded Holmes" of the Sandersonville Police Department came home to a hero's welcome. The moment he arrived at his office the goldfish swam to the side of the aquarium where it was usually fed. Harriet gave him a howdy wave with her free hand, the other on a phone and the four detectives in the office gave him something that could have been called a nod. Others would have called the response to his appearance as the nonverbal equivalent of "good morning."

So much for the welcome home, thought Noonan.

Then he looked at the mail piled on his desk.

"Welcome home" he snarled to himself.

As he was sifting through the mail, Harriet came over and handed him a postcard. It was in a plastic bag. "His Majesty beat you home by a day. He's been on all the channels."

Noonan shook his head. "What's he saying now?"

"He's claiming he solved the alleged terrorist bombing all by himself. Claimed he was the brains behind the entire operation."

"Of course! He's the East Coast epitome of a Texas sure shot."

"I'm not familiar with the term," Harriet said as she rolled her eyes. "But I'm sure it's a doozy."

"A Texas sure shot is an old expression,. . ."

"From Texas, I got that much." Harriet smiled.

"Yes, from Texas. It describes a person who shoots at the side of a barn and then draws bull's eye around where the shots hit. When the paint dries, he has a perfect record of bull's eyes."

"I've got to remember that. By the way, thought you might like this," she said.

Noonan looked at her strangely. "Why the plastic bag?"

"It could be evidence," she said as she crossed her eyes to give the impression of a lunatic. "It's from East St. Louis."

Noonan took the plastic bag from her hand. The adhesive stamp had an East St. Louis postmark. His name and address handwritten on the address side along with some poetry.

> I've labored long and hard for bread,
> For honor, and for riches,
> But on my corns too long you've tread,
> You fine-haired sons of bitches.

—*Black Bart,* 1877

"I looked up this Black Bart fellow," Harriet started to say.

"Oh, I know all about Black Bart," Noonan replied. "He was a stagecoach robber in the California goldfields. Robbed Wells Fargo. Never killed anyone. Got caught because of a laundry-mark on a handkerchief."

"You know your history."

"No, I read a lot of history."

He flipped the card over. The front of the card was the Egyptian figure of Seth, a humanoid with the face of an aardvark, squared rabbit ears and an erect forked tail. He was supported by a staff and held an ankh in his left hand.

"It's Seth," Harriet said. "I looked him up. He's the Egyptian god of chaos, confusion, storm and wind. From the news account that's what was going on in East St. Louis."

"Actually Seth is a bit more than that," Noonan said. "He is the Egyptian god of organized chaos, a concept the Greeks could not phantom. Something that is organized is not chaotic and the very definition of chaos is a lack of organization. But the Egyptians were clever. They understood life is simply organized chaos."

"Absolutely. Particularly around here."

Noonan popped the bag open and pulled out the card.

"Wait a second," Harriet said as she reached for the card. "That could be evidence."

"Evidence?" Noonan gave her an odd look. "Evidence of what? No crime has been committed. No diamonds stolen. No explosive device exploded. The terrorist is in the wind. No extortion. Just a very expensive bit of guerilla theater. Case closed."

He dug around in his desk until he found a thumbtack. He speared the postcard to the wall. "This is to remind me of the one that didn't do anything but got away with it anyway. A master of organized chaos."

www.ingramcontent.com/pod-product-compliance
Lightning Source LLC
Chambersburg PA
CBHW051642260626
47170CB00004B/1290